AFTER a token struggle, Belle surrendered to the Colonel's kisses and let herself forget everything else. Then suddenly she remembered that this was the same man who had ordered her off the premises, who had called her a tart!

"You have refused to buy me off, Colonel Gore," she said, "but will you be paying me for this?"

The Colonel had one last leisurely kiss and then looked at her with dark unfathomable eyes which gradually became contemptuous.

"I am afraid I expect rather more if money is to change hands. . . ."

The Girl
From the Diadem

Jean Merrill

FAWCETT CREST • NEW YORK

THE GIRL FROM THE DIADEM

Published by Fawcett Crest Books, a unit of CBS Publications, the Consumer Publishing Division of CBS Inc.

ISBN: 0-449-23752-4

Selection of the Doubleday Romance Library.

Printed in the United States of America

10 9 8 7 6 5 4 3 2 1

The Girl
From the Diadem

1

. . . *and Belle Barclay was on at the Diadem* in a piece of moonshine called *The Girl and the Garter.*

The Diadem wasn't Daly's or the Gaiety by a long chalk, but Lawton, who had taken it over when it was derelict and downtrodden, was pricking and goading it in their direction. Edwardian society adored the luxury and the obsequiousness, and found the red velvet and richly polished mahogany an imposing setting for the arrogant breeding of its men and the silks and jewels of its women. Besides, it was still considered rather fast to go to the Diadem, which was all the inducement the new era needed. Things were changing now that Queen Victoria had gone.

Lawton's shows provided in sauciness what they lacked in originality and probability. In the final moments of the last act, the Girl (Belle) coyly removed the opulent garter which, for some never-explained reason, concealed secret papers vital to a foreign principality's well-being, fell into the hero's arms, and then joined the chorus in some gibberish about Cupid's Darts piercing Princes' and Paupers' Hearts, and the something-something never will be free.

The curtains swished, the applause rang out. Old Joe Greatorex led Belle forward. Even with his dyed hair and painted face, he could still charm the birds from pit to dress circle. Mercifully, unlike Belle, his admirers couldn't hear his stays creaking in the love scenes. Magda Vasselli, sly and secretive, one of Lawton's unknowns, who was coming up fast, was on Joe's other side, Lucinda Varley de Vane (real name, Emily Stooks) came forward with Selina Summerton and Victor Slaney, the clever but malicious mimic. *Bit too clever,* thought Belle, who had never liked him. Anyway, there they were, all their little spites and jealousies tucked out of sight while they bowed and smiled and bowed again. The interior of the Diadem blazed into light to show what a giant's jewel box it was— "The King."

Pushing backstage, Belle Barclay realized how fatigued she was, and the sight of Daisy, her dresser, was no tonic.

" '*E*'s waiting for you," said Daisy, and from her tone, it could have been the Grim Reaper himself. "Told me to get out." Daisy's spaniel eyes, brimming with love and sorrow, were fixed on Belle for help, reassurance—anything. "I've got me flask," she said hoarsely, fumbling in some underpocket of her evening black.

"That *would* help," replied Belle. "Drunk, as well as done for. I shouldn't even finish the week." Then, seeing the abject misery in Daisy's eyes, she gave the thin, twisted shoulder a hard squeeze, somehow managed a smile, and walked quickly to her dressing room.

Lawton was occupying the visitor's chair. He didn't get up, not that Belle expected him to. She sank gracefully on to the stool in front of the dressing table and gave him a brilliant smile. Lawton stared at her as if he had never set eyes on her before, and Belle switched the smile off. No point in wasting it.

"You made a damned botch of the "Crybaby" number, you went to pieces in the opening chorus of Act II, and you made a *bloody* botch of that duet with young Slaney," said Lawton. "The rest wasn't much better either."

"I did not make a botch, damned or bloody, of anything," retorted Belle. "My voice wasn't too good tonight, I admit, but it's the dryness. London in an August like this is no treat. I've got some concoction which everyone swears by, so I'm taking that until my throat clears."

"That's more than Dudding says it will," contradicted Lawton.

They sat in silence, isolated in the brightness, part of and yet utterly removed from the babel that flowed past the door. If Lawton knew about Dudding, he knew about everything.

"My dear young lady," Dudding had said in his rich-plumcake, Harley Street voice. "My dear young lady." Much affected, he had sat beside her, holding one of her hands in both his own. "There are so many avenues open to us. So many roles. The legitimate stage, perhaps?" he hinted delicately.

"I can't act," said Belle wearily.

Dr. Dudding was horrified. "My dear!"

"I can't act," repeated Belle obstinately. "I can twiddle a parasol and flutter my eyelashes and drape myself gracefully against a gilt chair, an urn, or the leading man, which passes for acting at the Diadem. But that's all."

"I can't believe that a niche somewhere—" said Dr. Dudding hesitantly.

"In a Whitechapel sweatshop, perhaps," said Belle brutally, and was pleased that he instantly dropped her hand. "Well, what about my voice?" she had demanded. After all, she was paying a fortune for this. "It's worn out, isn't it? Worn out from years of bellowing across the footlights in music halls and number-three tours. It was never strong to start with, and now it's packing up on me. It's all right; you can tell me. I've known it to happen before." *And known what's happened afterwards,* she added to herself. One turned away from other people's tragedies, especially the tragedies of the once-successful. They had known it couldn't last for ever. They should have made provision for the rainy day. And, of course, no one ever did.

"Complete rest," murmured Dr. Dudding. "Nature's own panacea. Fresh air and sunshine. Absence of all irritation." He said "irritation" rather beautifully, and he repeated it admiringly. He had always fancied himself on the stage and his patients included a fair sprinkling of theatricals—of the better type, naturally, the actor-managers and top billings.

Too late, Belle realized her mistake in going to him. Dr. Dudding wouldn't dash 'round hotfoot to tell Lawton that his leading lady was vocally at her last gasp, but there would be a suggestion, a shade of nuance, a half-raised eyebrow, a discreet lowering of the lids, and the news would have raced round Leicester Square and up and down the Strand like wildfire, in one stage door and out at the next. "Have you heard about Belle? Belle Barclay! Poor cow!" And the inevitable, "Who will Lawton get now?" So while she was apparently at the height of her fame, queening it center stage at the Diadem, the gossips would have written her off and moved everyone else up a place. That was the theater—and life. She should never have gone to Dudding. *The Girl* was in her last week. A *holiday, the complete rest free from all irritation, and I should have been as fit as a flea again,* Belle tried to tell herself. *I should have had the lead in Lawton's next piece of mishmash (A Pearl of a Girl—*"Girl" titles being absolutely *de rigueur*) *and this would never have happened.*

But Belle's honesty, as usual, got the better of her. Dr. Dudding or no Dr. Dudding, Lawton would never have missed tonight's poor performance. She had got away with it, as far as the audience was concerned, through sheer professional charm, but not with Lawton. And no holiday was going to restore her voice for very long.

"You look like being a second Jessica Dines, don't you?" asked Lawton. "Her voice went, she lost her job, ran through her money, took to drink and prostitution and was finally fished out of the river. At Wapping, I think."

"Blackfriars would have been above her touch by then, I suppose," rejoined Belle idly.

Lawton stared at her uncomprehendingly.

"There is nothing organically wrong with my throat," went on Belle. "But Dr. Dudding will have told you that already."

"As a singer you are finished," said Lawton, rising. "I should strongly advise you to seek some other means of livelihood."

"Any suggestions?" asked Belle.

"I shouldn't think you would have much difficulty in marrying," considered Lawton, eyeing her from top to toe. "Providing you do it quickly." He made for the door. "I'm relying on you to take every precaution to get through these last three nights. If you can't, Vasselli will take over."

He went out.

So it was to be Vasselli. Well, the gossips would have that tomorrow. Belle glanced at the clock. It nearly was tomorrow. "Nearly Tomorrow, Today." That was the title of one of *The Girl and the Garter's* popular maunderings. *God, I'm sick of it all,* thought Belle, resting her chin on her clasped hands. *I wonder why I'm not crying. Here I am, facing ruin, not only for myself but poor old Daisy, and I can't even squeeze a tear. I suppose it hasn't sunk in yet.*

Daisy Sash, sidling through the door, stopped for a moment, breathlessly. *Beautiful Belle Barclay,* they had billed her in the old days, and although Mr. Lawton was too posh for that (always *Miss Belle Barclay* on the programs, give the old devil his due), she still had every claim to that title although—*well, she's in her late twenties,* thought Daisy loyally. Soft, white dimpled shoulders; a lovely length of neck which was always made much of on the picture postcards, when Daisy swept the thick coils of deep golden hair up and up into a dazzling erection embellished with fake jewels, flowers and aigrette plumes. Belle was considered too small to be one of the accredited reigning beauties but, like Gilbert's Private Willis, she was "generally admired." She was able, too, to rely on her perfect figure and reject the fashionable tight-lacing here and padding there, Nature having thoughtfully done it for her. As always, Daisy wondered why the Good Lord should give some women, like Belle Barclay, bodies of goddesses and others, like Daisy Sash (*who wasn't* that *much older,* thought Daisy) just working apologies for the same.

Sensing Daisy's presence, Belle lifted her head and gave a wan smile. The coarse theatrical make-up, now caked and stale, only served to emphasize the delicate modeling of her face and the warm velvety eyes under thin flyaway eyebrows.

Won't have much difficulty in marrying, provided you do it quickly, repeated Daisy to herself. *Flaming sauce!*

"The old B," she said, coming forward, a little black cockroach of a woman, with a heart as big as the Tower of London.

"Well, you can't run a theater on has-beens," said Belle, sitting up and stretching.

" 'Oo said you're a 'as-been?" demanded Daisy. " 'Oo said that? Did 'e?" Daisy's aspirates came to grief when she was emotionally disturbed.

"I'm saying it of myself. Now do shut up, Dais, I've had enough."

Daisy rebelliously started to unhook the Girl's blue satin, with a short, violent jerk to each hook. "You should never have gone to that old quack," she muttered as she unfastened the last hook and let the gown whisper to the floor.

"No, it was a waste of money," agreed Belle. "I could have told myself what he did. Ah, well, Lawton's tumbled to it and sent me packing, as I suppose you gathered from your well-known station at the keyhole. Your mixture's no good. I'm trying a bottle of Mother's Ruin tonight, instead."

"You ain't," contradicted Daisy. "There's a lovely young gentleman waiting to take you out to supper at Dulcimo's. There! Guess who!"

"Oh no!" groaned Belle. "Tell Clobber to get rid of him, there's a good girl. I can't face supper, Dulcimo's, or him, whoever he is. Clobber will have to regurgitate his tip."

"You'll have to go," cried Daisy. "You can't give in now. Put a face on it, Belle. Let 'em see you enjoying yourself, even if you *ain't!* Old Pickle Face always goes to Dulcimo's. Let him see he's not the only pebble on the beach and you've got plenty of nobby friends to back you up. You know what a thundering snob he is!"

"Who is this nobby friend then?" asked Belle. After all, there *was* something in what Daisy said.

"The Earl of Orsett," said Daisy. "All done up like a dog's dinner. Lovely young gent. Ever so good-looking.

The one who's in the Guards. Ever such lively young friends he has."

Belle vaguely remembered him. It was the fashion for groups of young Guards officers to descend on musical-comedy theaters and sweep the actresses and chorus girls off to supper, and high times were had by all. Lord Orsett, Belle recalled, was only marked off from the general run by being perhaps taller, fairer and even more charming than the average. However, she had never been met by him alone and was in no mood for a flirtation.

"Look, Daisy, you'll have to get rid of him. I'm tired. I must rest. I've three more performances to get through without actually disgracing myself. Send him off!"

Daisy stood, all aggressive and arms akimbo, breathing heavily, and Belle sighed. This meant a fight, and Belle hadn't the strength for it. She cleaned off her acting face and then, through force of habit, lightly applied her ordinary face. A dusting of powder, a smoothing of lip salve. Cosmetics were not approved of, and offstage, had to be treated with the utmost caution. She frowned at herself and put on another layer.

Daisy beamed. "You're going then? That's right. You won't regret it, Belle. He's a nice lad, stinking with money and he's got all the right relations. His uncle's that lovely gentleman what won the V.C. out in South Africa and who's standing for Parliament, so Clobber told me. His ma's right out of the top drawer and his granny's a duchess."

For one who came, literally, from the gutter, Daisy's approval of the aristocracy would have done credit to the crustiest Tory peer enshrined in the Athenæum.

Resigned to her fate, Belle obediently allowed a jubilant Daisy to drop over her head a confection of mauve frills and flounces, with a deeper mauve velvet cloak to cover it.

"There now, you look lovely," admired Daisy. "Don't tire yourself. Save your voice. Let him do the talking.

Look through Pickle Face if he's there, just like you did in *The Girl in the Gondola*. I'll clear up here and then get home. I'll wait up for you. Hold your head up and don't worry about me. There's always my sister in Hoxton, if the worst comes to the worst."

"You're a good soul, Daisy," said Belle, "and you shan't go groveling to that cat for the share of a bed. I'll go on the streets first."

"Well, we'll think up something. Off you go. Enjoy yourself!"

Belle moved gracefully to the stage door where Clobber was pigeonholed in his little grated nook. Clobber, who was reputed to have made a fortune from the tips he had received from stage-door johnnies. Clobber, who by some primitive instinct, knew to a nicety at what point on the social scale you were and tempered his demeanor accordingly.

Belle tried to analyze her own place from the look in his little piggy eyes and his half-salute. Ambiguous. He had obviously sensed that she was on the way down. On the other hand, there was a young sprig waiting outside and prepared to wait all night as far as Clobber could see. For everyone else had gone long ago, everyone who was liberal with his sovereigns and whose remoter family ramifications Clobber knew better than his own.

Watching him in those few seconds, Belle realized just how much was at stake, for Clobber was a true arbiter of her entire circle. At the moment things remained at *status quo,* but a feather on the wrong side of the balance and she would be finished.

"Young gentleman waiting outside, Miss Barclay," said Clobber.

"Yes. Good night, Clobber."

"Good night, miss."

Outside it was deliciously cool. It had been raining, for there was a dampness in the air and the tired London pavements were sweetened and refreshed. Patiently waiting by a hansom cab, and dressed, of course, in full evening attire, the gaslight shining down on his fair hair, was the Earl of Orsett. He came forward, his pleasant face beaming with admiration. "Oh, Miss Barclay, you are a darling to have come! You look wonderful!"

He held her hand a fraction longer than was necessary and then helped her into the cab. He sprang in after her and they were off, harness bells merrily jingling, the horse, a young one, banging his hoofs down as if he enjoyed the outing. Belle was so pleased it wasn't a tired old hack. She felt that she couldn't have borne that, tonight of all nights.

"It's awfully good of you to come," babbled Lord Orsett. "I particularly wanted to talk to you, Miss Barclay. It's—well, it's a matter of life or death to me!"

2

If by some paradox, discretion can be positively shouted, then Dulcimo's not only shouted it, but stood on a barrel to do so. The entrance was unremarkable but, even at that point, there was the quietness which always accompanies true wealth. Candlelight softened; the shadows concealed; waiters were noiseless; talk was subdued and mysterious. The making of an engagement for croquet on Thursday in Dulcimo's assumed the proportions of a secret alliance. There were rooms above the restaurant, it was rumored, where beds could be let down from the walls. There, ladies' maids waited to attend upon the Edwardian beauties, who, like great Spanish galleons in their finery, could not be boarded without a struggle and whose preparations for, and refurbishings after, a mild dalliance, took a considerable time. The gentlemen considered it all worthwhile, and certainly

these women were as lusciously, artifically feminine as
the sex would never be again if this new Women's Suf-
frage gained its way. Belle thought of it as the last, mon-
strous hothouse blossoming which should have died with
the passing of the nineteenth century but which, by reason
of some God-given St. Luke's Summer, had triumphed
past all belief in a last blaze of glory before the frosts
came. *Let's enjoy it then,* Belle had thought. But that was
before her voice started playing tricks on her and before
the visit to Harley Street. Now, she wryly assumed, as
the down-and-out which she seemed destined to be, the
sober, unattractive socialist world would be far kinder
than the exotic, aristocratic Eden which she had been entertaining for the last few years. Ah well! Tonight was her
last fling!

The warm, pink-shaded interior of Dulcimo's received
and swallowed her up, but not before Lawton had seen
her. She swept by him unheeding and was glad she had
come. She and Lord Orsett sat in an alcove, waited on by
one of the Dulcimo family in person, tempted with choice
dishes, refreshed by sparkling champagne, cossetted and
hovered over among snow white napery, heavy silver
and tight red rosebuds. At last they were alone. Lord
Orsett moved his chair around so that he was sitting close
beside Belle. He cleared his throat nervously and began.
Or tried to begin.

"I've always admired you tremendously, Miss Barclay.
All the chaps do, you know. Why, old Tubby Arbuthnot
said he'd like—well, he said he liked you very much. I
wish I'd brought Tubby. He offered to tell you himself.
He said I'd make the deuce of a mess of it. He's my
oldest friend, you know. But, of course, I couldn't have
done that! You see, Miss Barclay, to put it bluntly, Miss
Barclay—I'm in love!"

He sat back and looked at her appealingly. Very young,

very earnest, very flushed. "I'm tremendously, hopelessly, head-over-heels in love!"

Now for it, thought Belle. *Now you go all motherly, my girl and gently head him off. Oh God! Why should this happen to me tonight? I want someone to mother me!*

"Dear Lord Orsett," she murmured. "You won't believe me, but this has happened to me many times before."

"Well, you're such a *brick*, you see," said Lord Orsett. "Chaps just instinctively make for you."

"Many times," repeated Belle. "I am older than you."

"Oh, you don't look a day—" broke in Lord Orsett gallantly.

"In experience," continued Belle firmly, "and I can promise you that this will pass. You will meet some nice, pretty girl, someone you have known all your life, probably a neighbor, but perhaps have never noticed before, and you will forget me completely. At least, I hope not completely. If there is always a fond remembrance, a *tendresse* for me, for my memory, I shall be content." She turned her head to finish the performance with a dazzling but tender smile full at him, and found her escort practically goggling at her.

"But—I *have*!"

"And I shall always have the fondest thoughts of you," cooed Belle.

"No, no," contradicted Lord Orsett. "I mean I *have* fallen in love with a nice, pretty girl, and she is a neighbor, and I have known her for years, just as you said. And I want to marry her."

Belle could only imagine he had gone mad.

Lord Orsett managed a hollow groan and looked terrible.

"Miss Barclay," he murmured, in a voice trembling

with emotion, "I can only repeat what my friend, Tubby Arbuthnot, has said of me many times. I am a cloth-headed fool. He told me I would bungle this and so I have. I shall never forgive myself and I know you never will. I've a good mind to end it all," he finished violently.

"Lord Orsett," began Belle formally, "any apologies required to be made must come from me. My self-esteem is evidently so high that a gentleman has only to speak to me on some perfectly indifferent subject and I instantly assume that he is declaring himself."

"No, no!" cried Lord Orsett. "I mean, why shouldn't you? You must get proposals by the score. I know you do. Tubby swore that if he'd got a farthing of his own, he'd have proposed to you the first time he met you and damn what his old man said or did. I mean— I didn't mean that— I mean—"

"I think, Lord Orsett," interrupted Belle, struggling to keep her composure, "that you had better forget your friend and just tell me the story, for I presume there is one, right from the beginning. Why can you not marry this young lady who is an old friend and close neighbor, to say nothing of being pretty, without consulting me?"

"Well," said Lord Orsett, "you see, I'm in love with Julia. That's her name. Julia Sweeting."

"Sweet Julia," mused Belle. "With a name like that she is obviously the ingénue of the piece."

"She's the daughter of Professor and Mrs. Sweeting who live in Blackford Lefroy. That's where my place is, y'know. My family have always been friendly with them. They're very nice people, although there's not much money. Not that *that* matters," he went on hastily. "I've got enough to marry whom I like. At least, I shall have when I'm twenty-five."

"How old are you?" enquired Belle.

"Twenty-one next week," replied Lord Orsett miserably.

"Four years," sympathized Belle. "An eternity to wait, of course, and quite insupportable. Who holds the purse strings?"

"My uncle."

"Unsympathetic?"

"Dead against."

"On what grounds?"

"Don't say."

"Her parents?"

"Won't consent unless Uncle does."

"But compliant?"

"Definitely," avowed Lord Orsett.

Surprising if they weren't, thought Belle. Aloud, she asked, "How old is she?"

"Eighteen."

"How about a runaway match and sticking things out for a year until the first infant arrives? That usually causes melted hearts all 'round."

"I wouldn't dream of such a hole-and-corner affair with Julia," protested Lord Orsett. "And she wouldn't agree either. She's the dearest, purest—"

"I'm sure she's the sweetest of the Sweetings," said Belle. "I'm only trying to help you. What do you want me to do then? Speak to your uncle and soften him up?"

After an astounded stare, Lord Orsett broke into uncomplimentary laughter. "My uncle is *Colonel Gore,*" he managed to say at length.

"The V.C.?" asked Belle, dim memories of Daisy's recital coming back.

"Yes." He laughed again.

"Then—what?" snapped Belle, beginning to feel unutterably bored.

"Will you have another glass of champagne?" asked

Lord Orsett. "No? Well, if you don't mind—" Refreshed, he began again. "You see the position, Miss Barclay? Julia and I madly in love, ideally suited in every way. The only fly in the ointment is my uncle. My father appointed him my guardian and trustee of the estate until I'm twenty-five. Tubby's old man is the other one, but he does exactly as my uncle tells him. Hero-worships him. Always has."

"Why twenty-five and not twenty-one?"

"My father was like Uncle Piers. Didn't think anyone under forty should be allowed out alone. Then they both always thought that I took after my mother and didn't know my own mind for two minutes on end, so that didn't help."

"What about your mother?"

"Didn't trust her either, not with money. And quite right too," he added solemnly. "No idea at all. My uncle handles everything as far as she is concerned. I get my allowance, which I can manage on while I'm single, and my mother gets a thundering big quarterly allowance and not a penny piece until the next quarter. She knows that by now. So do I," he added ruefully. "She can't help. Uncle would cut her allowance for a start. Father and he— brothers you know—tied it up between them and padlocked the estate. Padlocked it." He stared into his glass and seemed in imminent danger of falling asleep.

"What does your uncle intend you to do then?" asked Belle sharply. "Stay single until you're twenty-five?"

"Lord no! He don't mind me marrying. All for it. But she's got to be his choice. Someone with a fortune. One of those American heiresses he's got down at Blackford now. Ugly woman. Great nose. Name of Muriella Goldspink. I ask you! And her parents! I could tell you—"

"And how do you propose to end this sorry state of affairs?" asked Belle.

With a quick look round, Lord Orsett drew his chair

even closer. "We've worked out a plan," he said, somewhat nervously.

"We?"

"Tubby—"

"Of course, I was forgetting the redoubtable Mr. Arbuthnot. In that case, why call me in?"

"You *are* the plan," explained Lord Orsett. "It all hinges on you, Miss Barclay! Tubby thought of it. We were talking it over and Tubby said, 'Julia Sweeting's a damned decent little filly and I don't know what more your uncle expects, knowing you.' He does know me, you see, Miss Barclay. 'I should have thought he'd have been strewing roses along the bridal path to think you'd settled on someone who's decent, white and presentable. Good God!' said old Tubby, 'it might have been some chorus girl or other.' And it was then, Miss Barclay, that the idea hit us, and the fact that you're on the stage and such a good sort, and *The Girl and the Garter* is closing this week so you'd be free to come down to Blackford for the house party next week. Well, it's providential! Do say you'll do it! My whole happiness and Julia's depend upon you!"

By now his cheek was practically resting on hers. Belle caught a hazy reflection in a gilt-framed mirror of Lawton and his party preparing to leave. Lawton glanced in their direction and must have seen the pretty tableau. Belle swayed even closer to Lord Orsett and smiled dreamily.

"Next week is my birthday, my twenty-first. I told you," Lord Orsett was saying. "We're having a big house party. My mother you know, very keen on anything like that. Cricket match, shooting party, boating, dances, a balloon ascent. All the usual."

Belle, who had spent her twenty-first in a back bedroom in Islington, with a bunch of violets from Daisy as sole offering, nodded.

"I want you to come as my guest. That's the plan. That'll start 'em thinking. Especially my uncle. He don't miss a trick. We want it to seem as if you're—you know—interested in me. You'll do that splendidly because you're an actress. It's my bit that Tubby and I are worried about. I've got to make it look as if I'm getting very attracted to you. We thought perhaps you wouldn't mind my sort of kissing you when Uncle's about, so he believes it's serious, and he'll be so afraid I'll marry you that he'll simply *welcome* Julia and practically order us to the altar. There!"

"I suppose," commented Belle, after a pause, "that it has the simple merit of complete lunacy."

"Oh no, Tubby doesn't think so. Tubby says no elaborate plan is necessary. Just for you to come and for me to walk with you and dance with you and flirt a bit. A few times will be enough to start the old hens cackling and my uncle to get anxious. You'll knock the other women into cocked hats. Except Julia," he added loyally, "and she's a different style. No, they'll all imagine that I couldn't help falling in love with you. You're laughing at me!"

"Of course I am, you ridiculous boy! At least, I have squeezed a half-compliment from you, which is something to be thankful for!"

Lord Orsett stared. "But, Miss Barclay! It wasn't a half-compliment. It's true! You're *beautiful*. Everyone knows that. Even my uncle said you were what every man dreams about when he's stuck out in the desert."

"Your Uncle Piers! Said that!" squeaked Belle.

"He admires you. He's been to see *The Girl and the Garter* several times. Said to see you in that appalling play was like seeing Aphro-somebody slumming it in a four-ale bar."

"Aphrodite?"

"Probably, if she was all right. My uncle thinks very highly of you, Miss Barclay, but—" He got embarrassed and broke off.

"As long as I'm on the other side of the footlights?"

"We-ell—"

"You know," said Belle, "I don't suppose it has struck you or your friends that no woman, not even a chorus girl, wants to be considered such an appalling prospect as a bride that the former rejects of skinflint uncles are welcomed with open arms!"

Lord Orsett had the grace to blush.

"Oh, it's all right," relented Belle, taking pity on him. "I know. But how am I to join the house party? Your uncle can only tolerate me across the footlights. What about your mother? Will she invite me?"

"She'll be thrilled," pronounced Lord Orsett. "She's very easy. I shall tell her all about it, and she'll die with laughing. Anyway, she's a socialist. It's her latest craze, so she can't object to having *anybody*."

At this final piece of tactlessness, Belle burst out laughing, and on that amiable note they left Dulcimo's and drove to 12 Meadowgate Street, where Belle and Daisy lodged under the auspices of Mrs. Makepeace.

The full moon riding high over the city gave its usual glamorous coating of silver paint to the plain, gray, daytime facade, and the refreshing effects of the evening shower still left a lingering sweetness. Lord Orsett touched his lips to the back of Belle's gloved hand and stood bare-headed as she ran lightly up the steps to the front door which had already been opened by the watchful Daisy.

Belle turned to blow a kiss and was surprised at how much better she felt. She was looking down at a tall, handsome, aristocratic young man who was courteously standing in the street until she had attained the safety of the house. But, by some trick of the moonlight which cheated with facts and perspective, he became a mysterious figure, the motionless hansom cab was some stage property bound for who knew what adventure. Meadowgate Street was a theatrical backdrop full of possibilities and romance. Even Daisy's white face floating, apparently unsupported, out of the gloom, was a wax mask not yet impressed into either of the conventional caricatures —Joy or Sorrow—but about to be. Oh, yes, about to be!

"Come in do," scolded Daisy. "You look better anyway," she added, after a quick glance at Belle's glowing face. "It did you good, you see!"

"Not only did me good but led to another part."

"What?"

"For one week only," laughed Belle, "but working in extreme luxury. And what is more, old dear, you have a supporting role!"

"I've never acted in me life! I couldn't say a syllable!" screamed Daisy.

"Nothing to it," soothed Belle. "You just stick to your usual role of lady's maid to that wicked actress and seductress, *Belle Barclay*!"

3

To Belle's surprise, the invitation from the Countess of Orsett duly arrived and was read over and fingered reverently by Daisy fifty times an hour.

Inevitably, Belle had woken up next morning, all the elation of the previous few hours gone; she was miserable, apprehensive, tortured by stage fright at the thought of getting through the final performances. By keeping completely silent when not actually on stage and submitting to being guarded and fussed over by Daisy, she managed. By the time the final curtain came she was practically sick with relief, although she was convinced by now that she would never appear on the stage again and her future was dark indeed.

Lawton came up to her dressing room just before she left it for the last time. This time he remained standing.

"I'm sorry that our last week has been marred by some

unpleasantness, Miss Barclay, but I trust it will not affect our old friendship."

Friendship! She and Lawton! Belle gulped.

"I hear you are to go and stay at Orsett Park as a guest of the Earl?" continued Lawton.

Belle inclined her head.

"A charming young gentleman, although the estate is firmly tied up for the next few years, I believe?"

"Quite probably," replied Belle.

"I am slightly acquainted with the Earl's guardian, Colonel Gore," Lawton plowed on. "I understand there is a match planned between the Earl and the daughter of an American millionaire who is also staying at Orsett Park, which would have the Colonel's blessing."

"Indeed?"

"A Mr. Goldspink. Curiously enough, I am acquainted with him, too."

You would be, thought Belle rudely.

"He has fingers in many pies but he has certain theatrical interests in the United States. A very pleasant gentleman."

Belle smiled politely, and Lawton, finding no further excuse to linger, bade her a courteous *au 'voir* and, on terms of armed neutrality, they parted. Belle could read Lawton like a book. He was dissatisfied with her performance, as he had every right to be, and his immediate and proper inclination had been to discard her without another thought. However, if by some extraordinary chance she were to become allied to young Orsett, Lawton wouldn't wish to be on the wrong side of the aristocratic fence.

Belle blessed Daisy for having made her accept Lord Orsett's invitation to supper. Had she turned it down, she wouldn't be leaving the Diadem with all flags flying. Everyone knew that she had been invited by the Earl himself to attend his coming-of-age celebrations. It had only

needed Daisy to drop a hint (in the strictest confidence)
for the news to have gone through the Diadem like wildfire and, in consequence, even the triumphant Magda
Vasselli dared not crow.

Vasselli had been re-engaged for Lawton's next musical
comedy and so had old Joe Greatorex—so Victor Slaney
informed Belle. She had had to laugh at his cruel imper-
sonation of Joe struggling into his corset while bowing to
left and right, though she always uneasily wondered how
many laughs he got at her expense when she wasn't there.

"He hasn't taken you on again then?" she inquired.

"Not yet. Like you, I'm awaiting the Call. He likes to
leave a few on tenterhooks, don't he? I shall have to have
a straight, man-to-man talk with him about it." He
dropped to his knees and licked the imaginary boots of an
imaginary Lawton. "Trouble is, he caught me 'doing' him
meeting the Kaiser. He didn't think much of it. Could
you take me down to Orsett Park with you?"

But Belle wasn't being led down that particular alley,
neither was she confiding in Victor Slaney despite his
parade of being a fellow victim, and she laughingly ended
the conversation.

Meanwhile, Daisy had less than a week to prepare for
their junket into high life. Less than a week in which to
make over, wash, clean and press, steam and sponge,
every single garment which she and her mistress possessed
so that shame should not be visited upon them in the halls
of the mighty. She had borrowed trunks and had packed,
unpacked and repacked fifty times. Helped by a friendly
dressmaker's apprentice she had, by some feat of genius,
"run up" several new dresses for Belle out of lengths of
materials which the dressmaker's apprentice had come by
cheaply. In each case the material had been of too violent
or too wishy-washy a color for anyone to want, or something had been wrong with it. Belle herself had been
doubtful, but having seen a brilliant purple silk toned

down by an interlining and ruffles of palest tulle, she realized that she could without a qualm leave everything to her devoted dresser.

"I know it's a bit—*striking*," explained Daisy, "but, after all, that's what we want, don't we? His Lordship *wants* you to look like an actress, don't he?"

Daisy had, of course, been told the whole story. Her immediate reaction had been terror and a conviction that they would both be put in prison for false pretenses.

"We're not acting under false pretenses, Daisy. Don't be silly. We're sailing in under our own colors, that's the beauty of it. We're doing nothing wrong. You just don't seem to understand."

But Daisy did understand, as certain remarks showed: the one about Lord Orsett wanting her to look as actressy as possible for one. She would also say at intervals, "You're trying to do that gentleman out of the money. It'll mean jail, I tell you. It's fraud."

"I'm not trying to do him out of anything. It's Lord Orsett's money. All he wants is his uncle's consent to marry the ingénue and a larger allowance to do it on."

But Daisy still grumbled. "It's a cruel shame. A gentleman like that, fighting for his country and wounded, then to come home and be tricked by his own flesh and blood and you, who ought to know better having been brought up in a Christian household. You be careful you're not so sharp you cut yourself my girl. He's a J.P. as well as a V.C., and he'll soon be a M.P., they say."

"Quite a little alphabet, isn't he?" mocked Belle.

" 'E's a 'ero," maintained Daisy fiercely, h's flying as usual, "and you should be ashamed to think of 'im as anything different."

"Well, we've got the juvenile lead, the ingénue and now the hero," laughed Belle. "I wonder who will be the heroine?"

"Not you, miss!" snapped Daisy. "You're the villainess, that's what you are. The villainess."

"My wardrobe certainly proclaims me as one," said Belle. "I shall strut like the peacock in his glory. You're marvelous, Daisy. Now, have you everything you want for yourself?"

"Me new black," said Daisy. "I shall do, I hope. Coo, Belle, I'm that terrified. I've never been in one of those big houses. I shan't know what to do."

"Just follow the others. You'll have no position at all, I'm afraid, my poor Daisy. The maids and valets of the lords and ladies will all take precedence over you."

"Suits me!" said Daisy, and bounced off.

Belle breathed again having got Daisy off the dangerous question of money and Lord Orsett's uncle, for Belle had got it all worked out before she left Dulcimo's. She certainly wasn't going into this for the Earl's sake, or for the unknown Julia's, or for the prospect of impressing Lawton, or for getting a week's luxury board and lodging, or for the fun of it as Lord Orsett and his circle apparently thought. No, Belle had her eye on the main chance. *If* the Earl's uncle (who sounded hard-headed as well as hard-hearted) really did believe his nephew was in danger of being seduced by an actress, he wouldn't fall into a panic and insist on immediate marriage to the unsuitable Julia, as the stupid Tubby Arbuthnot thought. He would do the accepted thing and buy the actress off. How much she was worth in buying-off money, Belle didn't know, but she hoped it was going to be enough to set up as an exclusive milliner.

Millinery seemed the best thing. She wasn't hard enough to start up an employment agency, she couldn't spell well enough to take up the new-fangled typewriter. Floristry was chancy and meant getting up early. No! Millinery! Daisy was a genius at making hats and Belle suspected that she herself had enough flair to sell them. So, although quite unconcerned as to whether Lord Orsett married his Julia or not, Belle was feverishly anxious that Tubby Arbuthnot's plan should go right for her own sake. No effort should be lacking on her part she vowed. She even went to the unprecedented trouble of visiting the public library and consulting the invaluable Kelly's Directory on the locale of her impending visit.

Blackford Lefroy (she read) *deriving its name from its ancient possessors, the family of Lefroy, is an ancient village and parish pleasantly situated on an eminence to the south of the Black river on the road from Thatchleigh to Flitch.*

It then ran on about petty sessional divisions, rural deaneries and dioceseses, and touched lightly on Roman antiquities, a ruined abbey and a Danish entrenchment. The church, built by a Henry Lefroy in the reign of Henry II, came in for a lengthy paragraph, and Belle learned that the embattled tower contained—*five bells respectively dated 1630, 1645 and 1700. Two others were added in 1901, the gift of Col. the Hon. Piers Gore V.C., J.P.* (*Well, he did shell out occasionally then,* thought Belle.) *The church was restored in 1886 by the Fifth Earl of Orsett at a cost of £4,000 and in 1897 a brass tablet was placed in the church in commemoration of the Diamond Jubilee of her late Majesty Queen Victoria by the Misses Maltravers. The east window is a memorial to Winifred, wife of the Third Earl of Orsett; the chapel used as the burial place of the Lefroy and Orsett families has some very fine monuments to those families.* Belle metaphorically hopped over the recumbent knights, quartered arms of France and England and shields of Lefroy, Gore and Beauclerc. *The two windows in the chapel are stained and were placed there in 1898 by the Countess of Orsett in memory of her husband, the Fifth Earl.* The deceased padlocker of the estate, as Belle worked it out. *On the south side of the chancel and partly in the chapel . . . elegant memorial to the Hon. Beatrice Maltravers, sometime maid-of-honor to Queen Victoria and wife of General Benedict Maltravers, C.B., Grenadier Guards. In 1884 an organ was erected at a cost of £500 by the Duchess of Peckham to the memory of her former husband, Henry, the Fourth Earl of Orsett.* The Duchess of Peckham? Belle tried to work that out but failed. Anyway, dead and defunct grandparents wouldn't enter the lists, surely?

Then came the church sittings, the church register and the value of the living. It was no surprise to read that this was *in the gift of the Trustees to the late Earl of Orsett and held since 1897 by the Reverend Crispin Amelius Whiffen M.A. of Magdalen College, Oxford.*

After the Free Church (Nonconformist) came the Blackford Lefroy Workmen's Club, which was erected in 1890 *on a site given by Col. the Hon. Piers Gore V.C., J.P. for the use of residents in the parish and workmen employed on the Orsett estate. It has a library of 500 volumes and is also supplied with newspapers and periodicals.*

On droned Kelly's through the almshouses and charities to *Orsett Park.* (*Ah!* breathed Belle!)

Orsett Park was originally a mansion in the Elizabethan style. The greater part was destroyed by fire in 1831 but afterwards restored at considerable cost. It is sited in an extensive park of 800 acres and approached by an avenue about a mile long from the Thatchleigh Road. It has an ornamental piece of water. Orsett Court is a square mansion of brick pleasantly situated in a park of 150 acres stocked with deer, a herd of which has been maintained here for over 250 years. The Trustees of the late Earl of Orsett are lords of the manor and, together with Col. the Hon. Piers Gore V.C., J.P., and the Misses Maltravers, are the principal landowners. An abundance of pure spring water is obtained direct from Monks Hadham by the pumping works of the Thatchleigh Hundred Water-works Co. A complete drainage scheme was carried out in 1897 at a cost of £5,000 by the Trustees of the estate of the late Earl of Orsett. The soil is loam and gravel, subsoil gravel. Chief crops are mangold-wurzel, kohlrabi, turnips. . . .

Belle's pretty nose wrinkled. Neither was she interested in the National School, the Volunteer Fire Brigade or the Railway Station (Thos. Highbed, Stationmaster). The sexton was Theophilus Gotobed, and the parish clerk, Albert Culpepper, who also discharged the duties of carrier, going to Thatchleigh on tues and sat, and to Flitch on fri. Miss Tibbits was subpostmistress. Belle skipped on to the column headed *Residents.*

Orsett, Countess of and Orsett, Sixth Earl of: Orsett Park (also 20 Eaton Square S.W.)
Gore, Col. the Hon. Piers Henry Lefroy Lefroy V.C., J.P.: Orsett Court
Maltravers, The Misses: Balmoral Cottage
Sweeting, Professor T.E.: The Glebe
Whiffen, Crispin Amelius, M.A.: The Rectory

Other selected souls of Blackford Lefroy were listed under *Commercial* and kept in their plebeian places—cowkeepers, beer retailers, general jobbers, outfitters, grocers and threshing machine props.

Well, that was enough, thought Belle, reverently closing the tome. It came over pretty clearly that, apart from slight assistance by the Misses Maltravers, Col. the Hon. Piers Henry Lefroy Lefroy Gore V.C., J.P., and the Trustees of the estate of the late Earl (alias Col. the Hon. etc. etc.) *were* Blackford Lefroy.

Mmmm! thought Belle.

They were to travel down by train. Lord Orsett and his friends were driving, but there was not sufficient room

for Daisy and Belle. Anyway, Daisy was all against it—
"Nasty, stinking things!"—and Belle shrewdly suspected
that her conventional arrival by train and wagonette
would be quite enough stimulation for her fellow guests
for one day.

"I do hope you'll be there when we arrive, Lord Orsett," said Belle.

"My dear girl, we shall be there ages before you. We're
starting at some unearthly hour and Tubby's chauffeur
has allowed oceans of time for breakdowns. No, we shall
beat you easily. By the way, I think you'd better drop the
Lord and call me Hugo, and, with your permission of
course, I'll call you Belle. To make it as authentic as
possible, don't you know?"

They traveled first class, an unheard-of luxury, and
were received royally at the little station of Blackford
Lefroy by, presumably, Thos. Highbed, who led them out
to the trap and Grinley.

Grinley was a superior young man in plum-colored
livery. They bowled along through country lanes thick
with hedge parsley, kingcups, honeysuckled hedges and
fanciful grasses, with the birdsong and cricket chirrups
loud and clear. Daisy gave a gulp at their first glimpse of
Orsett Park which, upon Grinley's half-glancing round,
she managed to turn into a hiccup. Better be thought tight
than impressed! It was a beautiful Palladian-fronted edi-
fice with a great lake before it (the piece of ornamental
water, recalled Belle) which actually sported a couple of
swans. Except for the water with its marble surround, the
whole place was a bower of greenery. Through the imposing entrance of great wrought-iron gates, surmounted by
heraldic griffins, they went, along the curved driveway
skirting the lake to the enormous portico. They were
awaited by a personage who could have been Prime Min-
ister and Archbishop of Canterbury rolled into one, but
who must have combined the qualities necessary for both

offices in his capacity of butler to the Countess of Orsett. He in turn handed them on to a maid, who led them up flights of stairs and through vast galleries to a magnificent bedroom overlooking rolling parkland, hung with apricot-colored silk, aromatic with potpourri and altogether delectable. The trunks were brought up, hot water was brought in and the maid withdrew promising to return to show Miss Sash to her own room and to escort Belle to the Chinese Room, where Her Ladyship would be dispensing tea to such as were interested in half-an-hour's time.

"That means a tea gown," muttered Daisy, face furrowed with concentration. "Well, we're all right there, praise the Almighty! That lovely cream voile with the tear. Me and Peg have smothered it with that cinnamon lace, but be careful how you move because we've only had time to tack it in some places where it won't show. I think we're all Sir Garnet so far, don't you, Belle? Here, Belle, didn't that girl's dress *rustle* lovely and that saucy little cap with streamers down the back! Makes me wish I'd gone into service. There, they'd have kept me in the kitchen I suppose," she ended with a sigh. She was working all the time, helping Belle out of the tailor-made, pouring out the hot water, bringing cool linen towels, running practiced hands over the masses of golden hair, producing powder and lip salve and finally throwing the tea gown deftly over Belle's head. "Honest, Belle, you look like a cream puff," she admired. "You look good enough to eat. Take a look at yourself."

Belle crossed to the pier glass and flirted with her reflection. The liberal hot water and fragrant verbena soap, plus the excitement, had given her face a glow. The soft voile with the tawny lace suited her mood. Teagowns were loose and comfortable yet romantic. No wonder they were fashionable. There was a soft tap at the door and the rustling maid with the streamers reappeared. "I'll take

you down to the Chinese Room if you're ready, madam,"
she offered.

"Has Lord Orsett arrived?" asked Belle.

"No madam, not that I've heard of, and we always
hear his lordship come in that there old machine. Makes
a terrible din, it do!"

Justly annoyed with Hugo for his tardiness but reassured by the maid's soft, country burr, Belle followed the
streamers through a maze of galleries, corridors and stairs
and past doors by the dozen all embellished with neat
cards in brass holders bearing the occupant's name. They
were passing one door when it suddenly burst open and a
stout old gentleman bounced out and collided with them.

"A thousand pardons, ma'am," he said, bowing low to
Belle. "And to you, Mary," he continued, smiling at the
maid.

She bobbed a little curtsey. "That's all right, Mr. Goldspink. You're late for your tea, that's what it is, sir, I'll be
bound."

Goldspink! The American millionaire, father of the
heiress whom Colonel Gore was dangling, carrot-wise,
before his nephew's nose.

"Mary," said Mr. Goldspink, "you have it in one. Never
had English tea before setting foot in this lovely land, and
I hated it, but now, by Jupiter, Mary, I'm addicted! Yes,
ma'am—addicted!"

He turned to Belle and she saw that he was sandy-
haired and sandy-whiskered and, although no oil paint-
ing, evidently of an amiable disposition.

"This, I know, is Miss Belle Barclay," he went on. "I
have had the honor of seeing you eighteen times, ma'am,
at the Diadem Theatre. My daughter, Muriella, says I
should have gotten a discount! Now I'm going to escort
you down to tea so you run away, Mary." He pronounced

it Murray. "I saw that lanky footman hanging about in the lower corridor not ten minutes ago."

Mary tossed the streamers but sped off just the same.

"You don't mind, my dear?" asked Mr. Goldspink, placing Belle's hand on his arm as they moved off together. "My name is Goldspink, Cyrus P. Goldspink. I'm a plain, simple Yankee citizen and I wasn't brought up to enter an English lady's drawing room when tea drinking is in full spate, unaccompanied. I'm liable to fall flat on my face. And Mrs. Goldspink and my daughter are already down there, I guess."

"I think you're very kind," smiled Belle. "I was wondering how I was to brave the ordeal."

Mr. Goldspink laughed delightedly. "Well, I can't think it's any ordeal for you, but we shall see. There's the footman on guard as a preliminary intimidation to strangers, see?" Dropping his voice he murmured, "They're nice people underneath, I suppose, but on the surface they're devils. They'll try to freeze you out. There are no introductions, for instance. You're supposed to know everyone already. You're supposed to have moved in their tight little circle since babyhood. Eternal tarnation, Miss Barclay, this country of yours has a lot to learn. There, there," he continued, patting her hand, "I must calm down. My wife would say I was making a spectacle of myself. She's settled down like a duck in water," he chuckled proudly.

The footman flung the door wide open and, thanking the lucky star which had sent Mr. Goldspink to her, Belle advanced to great her hostess.

4

Sunlight slanted through the four tall windows of the Chinese Room. Presumably the hangings and furnishings *were* Chinese; the furniture was certainly bizarre enough, with its bulbous fronts and its quantity of black and red lacquer. The curtains were of brilliant yellow silk. Head-high, china or porcelain vases so translucent that they were almost glass, painted with almond blossom and exotic birds, flanked the walls, and on the low tables were matching shallow bowls containing one great water lily floating in solitary state.

In contrast, the majority of the room's occupants were as English as it was possible to get, either tall, pale and droopy, or four-square and weather-beaten. All being well-bred, the conversation continued as Belle and Mr. Goldspink entered but it seemed, to Belle's heightened imagination, to have taken a desultory turn.

The Countess of Orsett was sitting behind an array of silver, looking helpless. She vaguely waved a small teapot about, but little refreshment would have been forthcoming had it not been for a maid of forbidding aspect who hovered behind her. The Countess had been a standard, tall, pale droopy, but was now a plump, pale droopy. She didn't look as if she would prove a problem. In fact, she seemed overawed by Belle and broke into a little torrent of chitchat. Had Miss Barclay had a pleasant journey? Was her room satisfactory? If there was anything she must always ring. What a sunny day, was it not? Had Miss Barclay had a pleasant journey?

"If you will pour the tea, Lady Orsett," broke in Mr. Goldspink good humoredly, "I will take Miss Barclay to sit by the window. Those young jackanapes should be coming any moment now and I want to see them arrive. My glory, I could have walked it by now! What do you think of automobiles, Miss Barclay?" he continued, as they walked away. "Do you think they have a future? They've asked me to invest in a new company that's going to mass-produce them."

"Are you going to?" asked Belle, astonished.

"Yes ma'am, indeedy! I like my money in machinery and something tangible, as a general rule. As my wife says, I haven't a mind above nuts and bolts. That's my wife over there."

He pointed to a handsome woman, handsomely dressed, who was eyeing them with some hostility over the rim of her teacup.

"And that's my daughter, Muriella."

A sallow, sullen girl, gauche and awkward, in washed-out pink, sat in a corner, moodily kicking at the flounce of her gown with a large foot. There seemed nothing that Belle could say.

"Old Vinegar-Mouth there," continued Mr. Goldspink,

"is the Marchioness of Melton. Mustn't upset her. She runs society, for all she hasn't a penny to do it on. The Marquis is the broken-down racehorse. Those queer old ducks are the Maltravers sisters. The dithery gentleman is Mr. Arbuthnot, one of the Earl's trustees. The dark one, standing back, is Colonel Gore, the V.C. He's the other trustee and young Hugo's guardian as well. He's been staring at you ever since you came in," he chuckled, "though come to that, they all have. You've caused quite a stir, you know. An actress friend of the young Earl's! They don't know what to make of that!"

And neither do you, thought Belle. She wondered if their meeting had been quite so accidental.

"Have you known Lord Orsett long?" he asked.

He was obviously fishing to know just how she had got an invitation, just what the relationship was between herself and Hugo, but however friendly he appeared and however thankful she was to have found him to break the ice in this pleasant way, Belle betrayed no confidences. In any event, she was saved by the roar of ill-adjusted machinery, the frightened screaming of a horse and much shouting and cheering. Through the imposing entrance came three motor cars enveloped in smoke, or possibly steam; Belle wasn't sure which. Hugo and his party were first with Tubby Arbuthnot (whom Belle scarcely recognized behind his huge goggles and under his flat cap), doing his best to ram them from the rear. Someone had a hunting horn and was using it. There were some terrifying explosions, and the machines came to rest outside the Chinese Room; Mr. Goldspink had thrown open one of the long windows and jumped out into the drive, where he immediately fell into animated conversation with the intrepid motorists and was soon flat on his back underneath one of the monsters.

As everybody else crowded to the windows Belle,

partly in excitement, partly in an effort to make more room, lightly swung herself over the low sill and followed Mr. Goldspink.

It was a terrible mistake. The drop outside was further than she had bargained for and Daisy's fears about the tacking were not idle. Belle felt and heard the stitches giving in all directions. Without thinking, acting instinctively, she hurled herself into Hugo's arms. That was another mistake. Hugo had only just descended from his panting and boiling conveyance, but he responded enthusiastically with a bearlike hug and Belle felt the beautiful cream voile literally falling off her.

"Oh, Belle! I'm so glad you're here! If only you had driven down with us, though. We've had a wonderful run. Only four breakdowns."

"Five," corrected someone.

"Oh, I don't count that burst tire at Flitch. That could have happened to anyone. We averaged fifteen miles an hour, I reckon, not allowing for accidents, of course. Didn't we, Tubby?"

"Hugo!" hissed Belle, "my gown has split!"

With a panache of which Belle had not deemed him capable, Hugo took in the whole situation. Holding her even tighter, he said, "Oh Belle, I've been longing to see you again. Come on, let's get out of this crowd."

And under the eyes of the assembled company—even those of Mr. Goldspink peered out from under the Napier —the sixth Earl of Orsett practically carried the actress, Belle Barclay, away from the group of his noble relations and welcoming friends to a secluded door, half-hidden under a rambling rose, which opened into a cool, stone-flagged garden room.

"Made it!" said Hugo. "I say," he added in tones of awe, "it has split, hasn't it?"

He eyed her with considerable interest. Belle tried to look affronted, but giggled at the last moment instead.

"What a good start! We couldn't have arranged it better if we had planned for a fortnight," exulted Hugo. "Now, which room are you in?"

"The Orange Room," said Belle.

"That hole!" exploded Hugo. "No one else will have it. It clashes with their coloring or something. And the bathroom's miles away. I'll soon have you out of there."

"No, Hugo, please!" begged Belle. "It's paradise. Just get me up there before this gown falls off. Do you think anyone saw it?"

"I'm sure they didn't," Hugo said enthusiastically. "You managed it wonderfully. No, they just thought you—well, what anyone would think!"

He led Belle by deserted staircases to the Orange Room then, promising to send Daisy to her, sped off, all excitement, to get back to the main party and find out the general reaction.

Daisy's alarm was such that if she could have found her way out of Orsett Park, she would have gone instantly. She set about reinforcing the evening dress which Belle was to wear that night so that it would have withstood the advances of a sex-starved gold miner. It was a sheath of violet silk, the back fanning out to form a tiny train. A matching ostrich feather fan went with it and Daisy had arranged with the maid that a posy of pink rosebuds should be brought punctually at eight P.M., so that they could be incorporated into Belle's coiffure which was scheduled to commence at that exact moment, dinner being at eight-thirty P.M. A "collar" such as the Queen loved—though, alas, of rose quartz, not diamonds—was brought out as a smart adjunct.

Once over her fright, and having received no peremptory summons to leave Orsett Park instantly, Daisy found that she had plenty of news. Her own room in the attic was spacious and sunny and was shared with one other lady who was maid to an elderly, several-times-removed

Orsett cousin. Then she had been introduced to the stewards' room and the servants' hall and had made the acquaintance of a Mr. Nabbs, who was ex-batman and
now personal servant to Colonel Gore, and who happened to be present, kicking his heels and waiting for the
Colonel. Daisy had so far entered into the spirit of the
thing as to attempt a chat with him on masters and mis-
tresses in general, to see if anything might be learned of
interest to Belle, but found him "blinkin' hard going."
She had, however, developed an admiration for Mr.
Sledgeman, the imposing first footman. She had also
been befriended by the maid with the streamers whom, it
transpired, was the daughter of the Albert Culpepper currently spoken of so highly by Kelly's, and his lady wife, a
former head parlormaid at Orsett Park. Already an invitation had been extended and accepted for Miss Sash to
take tea with Mrs. Culpepper on her first available
afternoon. It was always a source of amaze-
ment to Belle that she herself should excite any curiosity
or envy, let alone enough for Daisy to bask in as well, but
she was pleased that her faithful attendant was finding her
feet so quickly.

Daisy's recital outlasted Belle's toilette, which took
hours. First Belle had a great luxury. A bath in a real
mahogany-paneled and cerulean-tiled bathroom, and as
she soaked in the suds and steam she laughed aloud at
the memory of the torn dress and the stupefaction of the
house party. By the time she was dressed she felt ready
to face the lot of them, and when the dinner gong
sounded, she was impatient for the meal.

"How you've got the nerve to go down again, I don't
know," marveled Daisy. "Mary Culpepper said they
thought the old Marchioness of Melton would have a fit
and Bridgers, Her Ladyship's maid, overturned the tea
urn and scalded the pug's paw, and there wasn't half a

carry-on. They had to take the Misses Maltravers home in the landau."

"You're taken on your own evaluation, Daisy dear, and I'm going to value myself pretty highly this week, broken-down songstress though I am."

But, as she had guessed she would be, Belle was last in the pecking order for dinner. She was taken in by the least, the youngest and the poorest of Hugo's friends, a Captain Studholme. Nevertheless, they had a hilarious time together, and looks of censure or envy, depending on the age or temperament of the looker, were directed at them from the staider reaches of the great dining table, so loaded with silver and floral displays that there was hardly room for the food.

Captain Studholme had been told of the great plan and was full of enthusiasm for it.

"You've already frightened the old folk into fits, Miss Barclay, I can tell you," he confided. "They'll have their precious Hugo at the altar with Julia Sweeting before you can say knife."

Belle had by now become immune to the fact that marriage to her would amount to social suicide and merely asked if Miss Sweeting was present. Yes, she was, and Captain Studholme pointed her out. Through the wreaths of smilax, Belle saw a fairy-child, a drift of thistledown, rather surprisingly tucking into a quail in a workmanlike manner. She looked as if she should be fed on honeydew and drink the milk of Paradise, and Belle remarked as much to Captain Studholme, who was not literary and who seemed to be completely overawed at her turn of phrase.

The American girl, now in washed-out blue, very tucked and frilly, sat beside Hugo and stabbed discontentedly at her food. Hugo ignored her. He was concentrating manfully on resolutely keeping his eyes away from Julia and on Belle.

Between the nine courses, Colonel Gore, a martinet-looking man who could be imagined standing, sword in hand, at the top of some ridge littered with dead, and defying hordes of half-naked savages, screwed a monocle in his eye and glowered down the table at Belle and Captain Studholme, much to the latter's delight. "He's swallowed the bait! I told you, so Miss Barclay! He's taken it! Lady O will get the bullet as soon as he can get her alone. 'Who is this young person, eh? Eh? Who invited her down here?' " he mimicked in a hoarse, military growl. "Just look at old Tubby trying to keep a straight face! Lord, this will be the death of me! And the old boy was certain to have seen Hugo practically dragging you off the minute he arrived, without so much as a how-de-do to anyone else. That was a deuced good start, Miss Barclay, deuced good."

"Pray not so loud, Captain Studholme," begged Belle.

"Oh, she's as deaf as a post," said Captain Studholme, jerking his head at an inoffensive little woman on his other side—the elderly cousin, several times removed? "She's happy as long as she's eating. Whenever I've been down here before I've been landed with her. Swore I wouldn't come again. Never dreamed I'd have *you* as my partner, Miss Barclay. Miss Barclay, you look stunning, did I tell you?"

"No, but I don't need telling tonight," laughed Belle. "I feel it. It's the excitement and the feeling of danger I think. It always brightens me up. Otherwise I'm quite plain and dull."

"Are you?" enquired Captain Studholme with interest. "You should join the Guards, then. We have plenty of excitement. Of course, the South African war's over now. Dashed nuisance just when we thought we was going, but I suppose there'll be another good scrap somewhere before long," he added cheerfully. "There's always India, anyway."

"You are making the army your career, are you, Captain Studholme?" inquired Belle.

"Lor' yes, nothing else I can do," returned her neighbor with refreshing candor. "Hugo now, he's only playing at it. If he was twenty-five instead of twenty-one this birthday, he'd certainly have got his discharge because he'd be running the estate. Full-time job. As it is, his uncle's got the whip hand."

"But Colonel Gore himself has been abroad until recently," objected Belle. "He went through the South African campaign. How did *he* run the estate if he was away in the army?"

"Well, he's a different type to old Hugo, and older, too, of course," explained Captain Studholme. "He's been the rounds, you know. Puts the fear of God into everyone and sends filthy cables demanding immediate replies and so on and the agents go in fear of their lives. Hugo's a good chap, but he couldn't go on like that. Old Fotheringay, he's the chief agent here, thinks the world of Hugo and can't abide the Colonel, but he'll hardly move off his chair if Hugo walks in. Just let him catch a glimpse of the Colonel, though, and he's standing to attention and 'yes sirring' and 'no sirring' and 'it shall be attended to at once, sirring,' all over the place."

"And what does the Colonel say?"

"Doesn't say anything. Just strokes his moustache or sticks that monocle in his eye."

"He sounds horrible," said Belle.

"No, he isn't!" cried Captain Studholme indignantly. "Jolly good chap. Look how he won the V.C. 'Led his squadron across country and made a night attack with the bayonet on one of the enemy trenches. In the hand-to-hand fighting which followed he was badly wounded but advanced under heavy crossfire to capture the guns. Services rendered far in excess of those laid down by military regulations,' it said in the citation."

But Lady Orsett was rising. The gentlemen were rising. " 'Displayed intrepid courage and his personal coolness inspired the greatest confidence in his men' " got in Captain Studholme as the doors of the dining room were flung open. Belle brought up the rear of the calvacade of brocade, gold tissue, tulle and diamonds, convinced that she would never understand men.

5

The Great Drawing Room was stuffed with grand pianos draped with Indian shawls, brocaded sofas, velvet footstools, Japanese screens, enormous, terrible portraits of (it was to be hoped) dead and gone Orsetts, Lefroys, and Gores, tables covered with silver-framed photographs, splendid carpets, glittering chandeliers, three pug dogs and innumerable knickknacks. The ladies sailed in and with much rustling and fanning, for it was a very warm night, settled themselves elegantly and reached for their embroidery so that they could complain of never having a spare moment. The embroidery invariably consisted of a spray of anemic roses, which knew they were doomed never to blossom in their silken glory on this earth unless some poor relation or underpaid companion took pity on them.

Belle found herself a windowseat. It was dark but the

curtains had been left undrawn, presumably to give some illusion of coolness. Large, pale moths fumbled against the glass.

"Well, Constance," began Old Vinegar Mouth, the Marchioness of Melton. "Now that our host and his *friends* have arrived, I suppose the festivities will commence in earnest. I only trust they will not get out of hand." She raised a lorgnette and glared at Belle through it. "When exactly is Hugo's birthday?"

"On Friday," twittered Lady Orsett. "I do so hope that it is fine because the tenant farmers and all their work-people will be coming and there is to be a fair and a cricket match and a luncheon, although that of course will be in a marquee. Still, with the children's sports and so on, it's so depressing if it's wet."

"I see no reason why the fine weather should not hold," remarked the Marchioness graciously. "No reason at all," she added in the tones of one who would see what she could do about it. "And then the Grand Ball at night. Will the dear Duchess be coming?"

Yes, the dear Duchess would be making the effort. Over ninety now and went out rarely but still very sharp, oh yes, very sharp indeed. Mental faculties not in the least impaired. Sight and hearing excellent.

"Really too excellent at times, one feels," murmured the Marchioness.

Belle got the impression that the Marchioness was in some awe of the ninety-year-old Duchess who, measured by such a yardstick, must indeed be a positive Borgia.

"And the dear Princesses?"

Yes, the dear Princesses were to be there, accompanied by several sections of Debrett. The Marchioness nodded approval.

"Tomorrow there is the balloon race," continued the Countess. "The balloons have arrived, I believe. Several quite famous aeronauts are taking part and there is to be a prize and challenge cup presented by Hugo. He was infatuated with balloons a few months ago when the idea was first mooted, but now he has transferred his passion to horseless carriages!"

"Let us hope it is only to horseless carriages," muttered the Marchioness.

"And in the evening there is the Masked Fancy Dress Ball!"

All the young ladies squeaked with excitement and refused to tell one another of their costumes.

"We keep our masks on until midnight, and then we take them off," explained the Countess.

"Let us hope that is not all that comes off," said the Marchioness, fixing her lorgnette on Belle.

"On Wednesday we are having an expedition to Malthurst Abbey," continued Lady Orsett who had now consulted a tiny notebook in a gold cover. "The ruins, you know. A celebrated beauty spot. In the evening we are having a concert in the grounds. Tetrazzini is coming down."

"Quite a respectable little woman, I believe," conceded the Marchioness. "But, of course, the legitimate stage does have its reputation to keep up."

"Thursday is the first," hurried on Lady Orsett. Belle's was the only blank face. "And in the evening we dine with the Colonel."

She seemed apologetic about this and the news certainly awakened no enthusiasm in any female breast. In fact, one young lady remarked audibly that she feared she would be too done up after following the guns (the *guns*— of course, September first began the partridge shooting season) for *miles,* my dear, to go out at all in the evening. Several others said that they really couldn't either, they would be the dullest of company.

"Oh *please*," begged Lady Orsett. "*Please* come! He will be so offended. You can't imagine how difficult he will be!"

This prospect alarmed everyone and the incipient rebellion was crushed.

"Very well, very well, Constance," snapped the Marchioness. "As the boy's guardian he naturally wishes to do the right thing and give a dinner party on the eve of the day. The Colonel always knows his duty and it's up to us to know ours," she finished fiercely, and even the most sullen young lady straightened her shoulders and resolved to do or die at the Colonel's dinner table.

"Now, where are the men?" demanded the Marchioness. "I should not have thought they would have lingered tonight with such *fair* company awaiting them."

"Let's have some music then," said someone, and one of the girls twirled 'round on the piano stool and broke into a lively mazurka with the loud pedal full on.

Several of the younger ladies hopped about, practicing new steps, and their elders began talking animatedly amongst themselves. Nobody spoke to Belle, but she spent her time happily enough by taking them all in. She now knew Lady Orsett and the formidable Marchioness of Melton. She also recognized several society beauties and personalities of the day. The Misses Maltravers were unmistakable. They were just as she had imagined them: tiny things, ridiculously alike, with mouselike paws encased in black mittens. Belle also knew Mrs. Goldspink, Muriella Goldspink, the deaf cousin and Julia Sweeting, and very soon she knew Julia's mama. Julia's mama was a depressing vision of what Julia would become in maturity. The silver hair had faded into mere colorlessness and the engaging naïveté of the girlish face had become irritatingly bland. Julia's mama's baby-blue eyes, however, had a shrewdness which Julia's did not, and never would, possess. Belle was able to observe them particularly as she caught them full on her. Not being ladylike, Belle did not look away; she stared back coolly and had the satisfaction of winning the trick as, after a little hesitation, Mrs. Sweeting tripped over to her.

"It is—Miss Barclay—isn't it?" she inquired. "You were pointed out to my daughter Julia, by dear Hugo— Lord Orsett, I should say. I hope you don't object to my making myself known, but I couldn't help noticing how alone and forlorn you looked. So out of things and nothing is worse on these occasions. I am Mrs. Sweeting. My husband is Professor Sweeting, whom everybody has heard of! So that is one thing we never have to complain of, Julia and I, knowing nobody. Our circle of friends is vast but our dearest friends are, naturally enough, the Orsetts. We live, you could say, next door. At the Glebe House. My Julia and Hugo—forgive me, Lord Orsett I should say—grew up together. They were always called the Little Sweethearts by the late Earl, who loved to see them playing so sweetly together, and now they are sweethearts in earnest. Hugo—Lord Orsett, that is—is devoted to her."

"She's a pretty little girl," broke in Belle as Mrs. Sweeting paused to draw breath, having rather crudely put Belle in her place and the Sweetings in theirs. Yes, those blue eyes were definitely watchful, and that was a determined jawline and a thin, mean little mouth.

"Pretty!" tinkled Mrs. Sweeting. "My Julia has been called *beautiful,* Miss Barclay, by some of the finest connoisseurs in the country. *His Majesty* often visits here, or did when Prince of Wales, for the shooting, and we all hope he will continue to do so when affairs of state are less pressing, and many's the time he has remarked that Julia has a perfect Botticelli face and he said she could marry where she chose!"

Belle could have countered with what the King, when Prince of Wales, had said to her, but decided to spare

Mrs. Sweeting's blushes. She contented herself with remarking, "Sickening for the King to approve, but not Colonel Gore, isn't it?"

Mrs. Sweeting's sugar coating hardened, but she replied in words which had all the hallmarks of having had a good rehearsal and much repetition: "Colonel Gore agrees with the Professor and myself that they are both children and they should wait a little longer. Youth soon flits away, Miss Barclay, as I daresay *you* have found. Lord Orsett has heavy responsibilities ahead of him and his wife will be expected to help shoulder them. I should not wish Julia to bring anything but dignity to such a high position. The world of the Orsetts is a very different world from that of the Diadem Theatre, Miss Barclay!"

With which squashing remark she moved away, leaving Belle to think it over. Belle duly thought. From this slight preliminary skirmish she had found that Hugo had an ally in Mrs. Sweeting, whom she would have pitted against a very tough adversary. What sort of stuff the Professor and Julia herself were made of remained to be seen, and the Colonel also would have to be weighed up, but of one thing Belle was certain. Let him but waver for an instant, and Mrs. Sweeting would produce a fully accoutred Crispin Amelius Whiffen, M.A., from his rectory, or from thin air if necessary, and Julia would be the Countess of Orsett.

"Good evening, Miss Barclay," a loud, nasal voice broke into her reverie. "I am Felicia Goldspink. You have already met my husband."

"Oh yes, he was so very kind as to bring me down to tea," said Belle, moving up for Mrs. Goldspink, who was a large woman. Upon her enormous prow rested a number of large diamonds as if laid out for inspection and sale in a jeweler's window. Mrs. Goldspink wasted no time.

"I suppose that ridiculous Sweeting woman has been

pitching you that old chestnut about her daughter and Lord Orsett being pledged to marry from infancy? I thought so. That woman feeds on romantic novels. She has no idea how the *real* affairs of the world are conducted. The final financial settlements have not yet been settled, but Lord Orsett will be marrying *my* daughter, not hers, or anybody else's come to that. The Sweetings haven't a cent and Colonel Gore would never allow his nephew to marry a pauper. Misery and social ostracism lie in wait for any girl—or woman—so foolhardy to think otherwise," said Mrs. Goldspink, fixing Belle with a meaningful stare.

Nevertheless, the old girl was frightened of the Sweetings, sensed Belle. *And of me too,* she thought. Quite patently, Mrs. Goldspink was dead set on becoming the mother of a Countess and didn't care who knew it.

"Is money so necessary?" asked Belle curiously. "Surely—" and she indicated their luxurious surroundings.

"Believe you me, these old families can always do with more," replied Mrs. Goldspink.

"Well, as Colonel Gore's candidate your daughter has excellent prospects," said Belle.

"An heiress always has excellent prospects," was Mrs. Goldspink's unanswerable reply, and the gentlemen arrived in a heavy aroma of port and great affability. Resolutely ignoring Julia, Hugo came straight over to Belle.

"Nobody noticed your dress," he whispered. "Tubby didn't realize, and he was as close as anyone. They all think—well, you know. Couldn't have been bettered. I've been chaffed a bit, but my uncle hasn't said a word. He's got his eye on me, though!"

The eye was much nearer than they knew.

"This must be your friend, Miss Barclay, Hugo," drawled a voice behind them, and there stood the Colonel.

"Yes sir," said Hugo, jumping up and turning scarlet. "Miss Barclay—er, Belle, allow me to introduce my uncle, Colonel Gore. Uncle, Miss Barclay."

The Colonel touched Belle's hand lightly. "Hugo will have prepared you for the treats in store, of course, Miss Barclay. Balls, balloon flights, expeditions to ruined beauty spots infested with earwigs, if I remember rightly, gargantuan luncheons and dinners, fairs and a cricket match. Shall we see you at that? Or will it be altogether too bucolic?"

"I'm very fond of cricket," said Belle.

"Ah yes; well, Hugo will be there in all his glory, so naturally you would be 'very fond' of it. Many ladies are, I notice. You must beg Miss Barclay for some favor to wear in your cap, Hugo. A *garter* or some such trifle," he added sarcastically.

Hugo was being treated like a halfwit schoolboy and was beginning to look like one. Belle decided to do something.

"I should like to go and see the balloons if they have arrived," she said, "I've never seen one on the ground."

"That's a splendid idea, Belle," cried Hugo with relief. "We've had nearly a dozen entries. They're all in the Big Meadow. It isn't far and it's quite dry, but you'll need a wrap."

Belle produced a length of pink chiffon and held it out to him.

"Are you sure it's enough?" asked Hugo doubtfully, carefully swathing it 'round her shoulders.

"Oh, I shan't be in the least cold," murmured Belle, swaying close to him and turning on one of her particularly ravishing smiles. This had the disastrous result of startling Hugo, and Belle saw the Colonel's moustache sneer triumphantly, but Hugo quickly rallied, and, tucking her hand under his arm, gave a quick look round the

room and said, "Come on, I don't think anyone will notice we're deserting them for a few minutes."

The pressure of his arm told Belle that he knew everyone in the room, except possibly the serious young lady
currently in possession of the piano stool and soulfully
plowing through "The Indian Love Lyrics," was drinking
in the scene. The Colonel barked—it could scarcely be
termed a laugh—maliciously, but made no comment.
They had actually reached the door before Mrs. Sweeting's clear voice rang out, "Oh, you're not leaving us
again, Lord Orsett?"

The piano stumbled into silence on "beneath thy
chariot wheel" and the excited, haphazard small talk,
which everyone had been engaged in, died down. The
Marchioness' lorgnette was already in place.

"We were just slipping down to see how the preparations for the race tomorrow were going," explained Hugo.

"Then I must insist that Julia come with you for a little
fresh air. She has been looking quite peaky all the evening," said Mrs. Sweeting. "Such a *delicate* complexion
cannot stand the heat like these *coarse* ones," she confided to her neighbor.

"I think I feel a little peaky," repeated Julia obediently, "and the fresh air would do me good."

Belle found this hilarious but nobody else seemed to
notice. They were apparently accustomed to Julia.

"She can come if she likes," returned Hugo, "but I warn
you, we're not dawdling about, Julia, and we can't
wait for you to get ready."

Tubby Arbuthnot gallantly leapt forward to deal with
Julia's tiny white fur bolero, which was magically produced by Mrs. Sweeting, but he was forestalled by old
Mr. Arbuthnot, who leapt between them with little
squeaks of distress and intercepted the fur.

"A-a-allow me, madam! I am sure, P-p-peregrine, that your studies—"

"Old Butty's terrified of matchmaking mamas," whispered Hugo in Belle's ear. "Still thinks of Tubby as a lad of fourteen. If he knew some of the things Tubby's got up to in his time, he'd drop dead!"

Belle could well believe it.

"Let's all go!" cried Captain Studholme, laughing immoderately, and in the resulting confusion, Belle and Hugo got out of the room and into the warm, scented darkness of the grounds.

"We're doing jolly well, you know," congratulated Hugo, putting his arm almost nonchalantly around Belle. "We needn't hurry. The others will hold things up in there. I'm a bit slow sometimes, but I think I'm getting the hang of it now. My uncle throws me a bit. He's always treated me as if I was weak in the head. Perhaps I am!"

"Of course you're not! Anyway, he'd throw anybody with his horrid sneering way. It was charmingly natural, and just how you would be expected to behave if you were really in love with me?"

"What did you think of Julia?" asked Hugo, who had evidently not taken in a word. "She's divine, isn't she?"

"Very divine. By the way, have you told her or her mama of your scheme?"

"Good lord, no!" exploded Hugo. "Julia would instantly trot off and ask my uncle if it wasn't a good idea! As for Mrs. Sweeting, well, I think it's more authentic-looking if she *doesn't* know, don't you think? I mean, very nice woman and all that, but dead set on my marrying Julia, and you can see that she's not taking it well. You coming down here as my guest, I mean. You can see she's not putting it on. She'd have a hard job to act as naturally as that."

At least, he's not so blinded by Julia that he can't see

that she's a fool and her mother a fortune-hunter, thought Belle. *That's something.*

"Apart from your friends, and I do hope they'll be discreet, only your mother knows then?"

"Yes, I promised you I'd tell her, and she's safe enough. She thinks it's all a lark. She's enjoying fooling the Colonel too."

Belle could hardly imagine Hugo, his friends and the Countess fooling the Colonel for long, but Hugo's faith seemed unbounded, so she said no more on the subject. However, she did say, "I have met the American millionaire and his wife. They both went to some pains to become acquainted."

"They would," remarked Hugo rudely.

"The daughter seems a docile sort of girl."

"Ugly."

"I don't know," considered Belle. "She's dressed all wrong or something. She's playing a part too, but very indifferently. There's something out of true there, but I certainly wouldn't call her ugly."

"Well, I would."

"And she could buy Miss Sweeting and me up out of her loose change. Oughtn't you to consider it more seriously?"

"I thought you were coming down to help me marry Julia! I don't see why you should suddenly go over to my uncle's side!"

No, neither do I, thought Belle, *except that you must be crazy to want to marry that piece of dandelion fluff.* Her sympathies were entirely with Colonel Gore and her admiration reserved for the percipience of Hugo's father. No wonder he had padlocked the estate when he had seen the Little Sweethearts at play! Still, she must watch out for herself. It wouldn't suit her book at all if Hugo did veer about and decide to marry Muriella!

"We're nearly there," said Hugo, and Belle came back

to earth with a start. "Look, you can see the balloons through those trees."

"I think," said Belle, "that we should walk in the opposite direction. Everybody will be hurtling along this way looking for us. I think we should stroll somewhere else and appear in, say half an hour, looking happy and dazed, and vague about where we've been!"

"Honestly, Belle, you are smart! I should never have thought of that!"

So the sixth Earl of Orsett and the actress Belle Barclay doubled back and wandered in an enchanted world of statuesque swans, classical temples and urns filled with pelargoniums and trailing ivy. Belle sighed with pleasure as they rounded the lake and started back towards the mansion, which was ablaze with lights. Then, not looking where she was going, she stumbled. Hugo, who had been very quiet, presumably lost in dreams of Julia, looked down and said sharply, "Good Lord! You're wearing silly satin slippers to walk over this rough gravel. Your feet will be cut to ribbons." And before she could protest he swung her up into his arms and carried her to the house, putting her gently and lingeringly down on the terrace. Guessing this was for someone's benefit, Belle glanced 'round. Sure enough, coming along the front of the house were Julia Sweeting on the arm of Tubby Arbuthnot (whose face bore a look of the most pious disgust Belle had ever seen), Mr. Arbuthnot clucking in an agony behind them, several assorted couples, the Goldspinks and—joy!—the Colonel.

"Hugo!" called out Julia in a piercing treble. "We have been looking for you. Has Miss Barclay spwained her ankle?"

"Come away, Miss Sweeting," begged Tubby Arbuthnot, rolling up his eyes. "Allow me to escort you to your mama."

"Did you see the balloons, Hugo?" asked Julia.

"No," said Hugo. "We walked the other way."

"But you wanted to see the balloons. And Miss Barclay wanted to see the balloons. And we all went to see the balloons. You said you wanted—"

How any man in his senses could contemplate marrying Julia, Belle couldn't imagine.

"Pray come into the house, Peregrine," begged Mr. Arbuthnot. "The night air—"

"Well, I can't understand it," continued Julia.

In the Great Drawing Room several bridge tables were going. There was a general welcome, and Julia was soon informing everyone of Hugo and Miss Barclay *wanting* to see the balloons and then walking the other way. "Wasn't it odd, Mama?"

"Very odd," replied Mrs. Sweeting, tight-lipped. "I think it is high time we returned home, Julia. You will have a late night tomorrow, you know."

"Ooooh yes! The Fancy Dwess Ball. Hugo, you must guess who I am or I shan't speak to you again."

Oh, be yourself and come as a Silly Goose, thought Belle wearily. Then, prompted by some demon of mischief (after all, might as well make a day of it!), she sank languidly on to the piano stool and ran her fingers over the keys. She sensed everyone stiffen and conversations die. Now what should it be? Oh yes! And she slid into that most charming of Sullivan melodies from *Iolanthe*, "Good Morrow, Good Lover!" After all, it was after midnight. She played prettily though not spectacularly and the song suited her light, pleasing voice. She played and sang softly, almost to herself, but was delighted at the effect she knew she was having. Hugo had the sense to come and lean on the piano and give her speaking looks.

> And join in a measure
> Expressive of pleasure,

> For we're to be married today—today!
> For we're to be married today!

No one applauded or spoke until the Marchioness said, "I think I shall go to bed now, Constance. I feel, I feel—*distrait*."

Then, in the general break-up of the party, Belle heard her hiss, "Constance! They *aren't*! *Are* they?"

6

True to the Marchioness' word, the weather held and next morning the sun streamed in Belle's window, rioting over the tangerine silk bedcover and draperies, over the dressing table with its exciting silver-stoppered bottles and jars and over Belle herself as she sat up flushed, yawning and gorgeous.

"I suppose you want your breakfast in bed," accused Daisy, jangling the curtain rings to emphasize her displeasure.

"Of course I do," replied Belle cheerfully. "Look sharp. Whatever's going."

"You'd *better* have it up here, madam," went on Daisy. "You'd *better*. Not even you could face that lot again so soon after your performance last night. Oh, I've heard all about it! Lucky I'm respectable meself, or they'd turn me out of the steward's room. I've heard about you letting

His Lordship carry you 'round the grounds *in his arms*, and Gawd knows what you was up to down by the lake, but even the tweenie can make a good guess, and then singing that song to him like that in front of everybody. I just tells 'em that you come from a good 'ome and I only stops with you because it was a deathbed promise to your sainted ma. Mr. Sledgeman said good morning to me," she added with conscious pride.

"There you are then," said Belle, "if you can't be aristocratic, be notorious. But *be noticed*!"

"I'll see what I can get," sniffed Daisy.

"That's an angel and hurry, because somehow we've got to concoct a fancy dress for tonight."

"You must be weak in the head," yelped Daisy, making for the door. "And don't get out of that bed. I don't want one of them young chambermaids to come barging in here and find you without a stitch on. Things are bad enough as it is. They don't know yet that you sleep in the nood."

She returned with a loaded tray of porridge, kedgeree, bacon and mushrooms, hot rolls and coffee—and a better humor. "Mr. Sledgeman asked if I'd got a regiment up here," she giggled, "and when I told him it was only you he nearly dropped the lot. He carried the tray. Said it was too heavy for me. 'Well,' he said, 'there's not much wrong with someone who eats a hearty breakfast and I hope she *does* marry His Lordship, so there!' 'What an idea,' I said. 'Well,' he said, 'we're taking bets on it and she's six to four favorite,' he said."

"There's your chance then, Dais," said Belle, tucking in with a will. "Get some money on that I won't, and you'll make your fortune."

There was a short silence.

"What you going to wear tonight?" asked Daisy, and Belle looked at her in surprise, for it wasn't like Daisy to leave a subject until she had not only worried it to death, but buried it too. "They're all going like blinkin' Chinese pagodas, what I can hear of it."

"I thought so," said Belle, between mouthfuls. "So I'm going all demure. Do you remember the dress I wore in that terrible play *Mistress Betty's Respects*? Dead simple. Muslin with that high Empire waist? Make me one like that!"

"You used to damp it so it clung," whispered Daisy. "I caught you at it."

"Authenticity," returned Belle. "Well, what about it? It's only for the evening, and there was nothing in it."

"For a start, where am I going to get the muslin, let alone the trimmings? For another, who's going to help? Because *you* can't thread a needle."

"There must be rolls of material about and scores of willing hands. Get me up and we'll see. Heavens! What about the balloon race?"

"Starting in about an hour," said Daisy. "His Lordship was asking if you would go down with him."

"I shan't be able to, but I must see him. Something easy to put on, Daisy dear. Quick!"

While she was dressing she learned that Daisy had not only got a good morning out of Mr. Sledgeman but that Mr. Nabbs, the Colonel's man, had of his own free will taken her outside and pointed out the Colonel. "A real toff and no mistake," admired Daisy. To retaliate, Mr. Sledgeman had shown her Mr. Goldspink, but Daisy hadn't thought much of him. Not that she would have done if Mr. Goldspink had been six feet tall with the looks of Adonis. Daisy was British through and through, and despised all foreigners.

When Belle was ready Mr. Sledgeman, who just happened to be in the corridor outside, running his finger along the undersides of the sills and ledges, guided her down to the main hall. A number of people were going off in little groups to see the start of the race and Hugo was looking at his watch anxiously. Julia, very fresh and dainty, was beside him. Belle ran lightly down the last flight of stairs and, as soon as he caught sight of her, Hugo abruptly left Julia and hurried over.

"Belle darling, I've been waiting for you. Come on!"

Several ladies nudged each other and Julia's lower lip trembled.

"I can't, Hugo," said Belle. "I've got to concoct a dress for tonight. I didn't bring anything suitable and you didn't warn me."

"It doesn't matter," frowned Hugo. "Not everyone's going in fancy dress. Besides, my mother will find you something or, rather, Bridgers, her maid, will. There's always something for anyone who's caught. Come on!"

"No. I have a fancy to do everyone in the eye," said Belle, "but I do need help. I want some material—muslin and silk—and a sewing machine and a sempstress!"

"I have a sewing machine," remarked a voice behind them, "and I'm quite good at making things. Could I help?"

It was the American girl, more unfortunate than ever in an embroidered pink gown and a little-girl sunbonnet. Her hair was in bedraggled ringlets.

"Miss Goldspink!" exclaimed Belle. "That's sweet of you, but I couldn't possibly allow you to give up your day. You would miss the balloon race."

"I don't want to see it," said Muriella. "I have no one to go with."

"Oh, I say—" began Hugo, belatedly remembering his duty as a host.

"But your mama—"

"She and Father have gone up to town for the day. I'd love to help. Honestly, Miss Barclay. I want to *do* something."

She spoke so sincerely, and there was so much unhappiness in her whole bearing that Belle felt downright sorry for her.

"Julia! Hugo!" called Mrs. Sweeting from the doorway. "Are you coming, my dears?"

"Yes mama," responded Julia, tucking her arm through Hugo's.

"But Belle—Miss Goldspink—" began Hugo, help-lessly.

"Off you go, Hugo," ordered Belle briskly. "I shall take advantage of Miss Goldspink's very kind offer. Enjoy yourself."

She gently turned him towards the door and patted him away. Giving her one furious look, Hugo moved on with Julia.

The American girl stared after them, Hugo so tall and handsome, Julia an animated little porcelain figurine. Her eyes were blurred with tears and Belle suddenly realized, with horror, that Muriella Goldspink was in love with Hugo. This was no piece of title-catching on Muriella's part, it was genuine adoration. To hide her embarrass-ment, Belle began talking volubly about the dress she had in mind. The Regency period, so delightful, didn't Miss Goldspink think?

"We shall want white muslin and silk for the lining," replied Muriella, making a valiant effort. "I'll get my maid to start the ball rolling. If you and your maid come up to my room in half an hour I will be ready."

With profuse thanks Belle tripped off to inform Daisy of the latest developments, and half an hour later they presented themselves at Muriella's door. A transformed Muriella awaited them. Gone was the voile, the sunbon-net, the ringlets. She wore a striking dress of black and white stripes with crisp white collar and cuffs. It was a spanking, snappy American creation. The ringlets were combed out and her hair was drawn straight back from her face into a large, uncompromising bun. She looked businesslike, smart and entirely different. She was, Belle realized, a good-looking girl with strong bones and an alert, intelligent face. Daisy and Belle, having gaped speechlessly at Muriella, then gaped at her room. For the first time since she had known her, Belle saw Muriella smile. And then giggle.

"It's the Orsett prospective bride's suite," she explained. "Hardly homey, is it?"

It was a vast white room. White carpet covered with white bearskin rugs, white walls covered with gilt-framed mirrors. A wall of windows with *eau de nil* velvet curtains. Luxurious armchairs in striped satin, and glass, marble and gilt tables were scattered everywhere, yet there was no sense of overcrowding. Beyond was Muriella's bedroom containing an enormous bed canopied in a mist of snow-white tulle, and on the bed lay a roll of pretty figured muslin and another of palest shell-pink silk. Orsett Park had dealt with Belle's requirements with contemptuous ease. Tape measures, pins, needles, thimbles, cottons, buttons and silks were all to hand.

"They have everything here," said Muriella. "It's like a small town. It fascinates me. They have tremendous storerooms and stillrooms and icehouses and cellars and larders and pantries and workshops and glasshouses and attics, even a smithy and a brewery. And someone terrifically competent is in charge of each of them and can find you whatever you want or do anything you want in next to no time. The Countess' dressmaker would have run this up for you, but I like making things, and if your maid will help, I'm sure we can get it ready for tonight. I want something to occupy me."

She was a fast, efficient worker. Daisy, wary at first, blossomed out and they worked well together—the American heiress and the cockney foundling. Daisy was allowed to use the machine and, although she tried hard, could not conceal her admiration, foreign though the device was. Always vigilant, Belle wondered if Muriella would take Daisy on if the worst came to the worst, but dismissed the idea hopelessly. Daisy would insist on starving with her mistress, and Muriella's own maid, a vast Negress, looked in remarkably good health and showed every sign of the strongest attachment to her mistress.

As she stood obediently in the middle of the room being pricked and pinned by Muriella and her two helpers, Belle saw the first of the balloons ascend over the treetops. It was a mythical sight, a giant puffball against the blue sky. In the basket were two men waving their top hats. Later some ladies went up, wearing large picture hats wound 'round with veiling.

Muriella ordered lunch on a tray and became more forthcoming than Belle would have thought possible. She talked sensibly and well of the running of Orsett Park, of the acreages, the outgoings, the welfare of its dependents. What a superb countess she would make! Belle, who had not hitherto considered the possibility, now became obsessed by it. Muriella Goldspink, once out of those miserable, clinging, little-girl dresses, was a force to be reckoned with. She had the profile of a countess! She had the competent, confident manner of a countess. Poor Connie Orsett was nowhere, nowhere! While as for Julia— Muriella would manage Hugo, manage the estates, manage the Park, manage the family, even manage the Colonel, decided Belle. She was the perfect choice, and only that silly little idiot, Julia Sweeting, stood in the way.

"What are you going to the ball as, Miss Goldspink?" she enquired abruptly.

Muriella became very occupied in measuring off a length of satin ribbon. "My parents have gone to London to collect my dress," she said. "It has been made specially. Mama chose it. It's a reproduction of one of the *Cries of Old London*. A lavender girl."

"Oh," said Belle, doubtfully, but if she didn't venture to comment, Daisy wasn't so reticent.

"Oh miss! You want something with more *color,* more life than tha' A lavender girl! That's all right for Miss Sweeting, not for you."

"That's just it," Muriella remarked bitterly. "My mother has seen the success Miss Sweeting has had with—with Lord Orsett, and she thinks I should emulate her."

"What a load of nonsense, begging your pardon, miss!" spat Daisy. "You look a hundred times better as you are now. You can't wear those milkmaid dresses that Miss Sweeting does."

"Well, my mama thinks it's my only chance of capturing an English milor'," said Muriella.

"Then your mama wants to have a look at the success my mistress has with His Lordship," declared Daisy. "And she don't wear no namby-pamby stuff!"

"Daisy!" expostulated a shocked Belle. "Miss Goldspink, I must apologize—"

"It's all right," said Muriella. "It's true. I think that even my mother will have to realize now that I don't stand a chance whatever I do."

"Sorry, miss," muttered Daisy in her turn. "It just seemed such a *waste.* Lavender girl, indeed! Haven't you got anything else?"

To their relief, Muriella laughed and brightened up. "When I came, I brought a costume with me for such an occasion. Here, what do you think of it?"

She sprang up and opened the door of one of the cupboards which ran the length of her bedroom. It was crammed with dresses, but Muriella unerringly pulled out a stunning creation in gold lamé. "I can't show you the headdress, that's packed away separately, but believe me, it's a work of art. It's enormous and made of feathers and diamonds. It represents a bird of paradise!"

Awestruck, Belle and Daisy drooled over the beautifully made tunic and trousers, looked at each other and then at Muriella.

"You'll have to wear it," decided Belle. "No matter what your mother says."

"Cor' yes!" breathed Daisy. "That'll make His Lordship look. Be yourself, miss. Sail under your own colors, do."

Muriella, far from resenting the free and easy way which Daisy was taking with her, seemed appreciative—and thoughtful.

"I wonder," she said. "I wonder."

7

The dress was a great success, and Belle looked,
as Muriella put it, like a cute doll. The white figured
muslin was demure but the wide, low décollotage was
anything but. Tiny puffed sleeves just rested on her
shoulders, leaving her arms bare but for long, loose white
satin gloves. The pink underslip showed through beautifully and they had made a sash and a scarf to match. The
sash was wide and fastened high, just under her breasts,
the scarf was threaded negligently through her purposely
tumbled coiffure, one end trailing on to a bare shoulder.
White kid slippers and a tiny pochette on a long, silver
chain completed the ensemble. Belle made her face up
delicately and adjusted the thin mask which Daisy had
procured for her. It was a little black feathery affair nowhere near as marvelous as Muriella's magnificently or-
nate golden one (for Muriella, to their delight, had

decided in favor of the bird of paradise, and Mrs. Goldspink had, according to the servants' hall, washed her
hands of her daughter forever), but Belle could have com-
peted with none of her fellow guests in terms of splendor
and she was well satisfied.

In the ballroom were half-a-dozen Marie Antoinettes,
ruffs and farthingales by the score, several lavender girls
(so much for Mrs. Goldspink's originality) and beauties
of the Court of Charles II coquetting in every corner.
Most of the men had taken to dashing, full-dress regi-
mental uniforms of long ago and, for once, outshone their
womenfolk. Hugo looked very swagger in tight scarlet and
gold braid, so did his friends. Belle knew all of them
directly despite their masks. It was something in the manner of walking, the turn of the head, the hands.

The medieval costume with wide fur-edged sleeves
could not hope to disguise the Marchioness, who stamped
about in patent leather button boots, blissfully indifferent
to authenticity, while Mr. Goldspink, in the costume of
Uncle Sam, publicized rather than disguised himself. The
Misses Maltravers had, under the auspices of the late
Queen Victoria, one felt, arrayed themselves in the Balmoral tartan with daring tam o'shanters to match. The
younger Miss Maltravers' had a bobble on the top, the
elder Miss Maltravers' had not.

Muriella was as superb as Belle had suspected she
would be and had attracted much attention. Even Hugo
had stared. With the change in dress had come a change
in manners, and she was, although Belle was pained by
it, rather loud and brash. Still, she was a hundred times
happier and more attractive.

The Colonel had disdained masks and fancy dress. *He
might have come as something,* thought Belle resentfully,
but the Colonel had work to do. She saw him mentally
tick off Hugo as easily as she had done, nod approvingly
to Muriella and scowl at Julia, who was a Parisienne

Bo-Peep. She looked adorable, but nobody would have trusted her with the staidest of sheep for a moment. Still the Colonel's eyes searched the room and Belle realized with a thrill of pleasure that he was looking for *her!* He wanted to know where everyone was and with whom tonight. She moved out a little from a Romney beauty. whose generous curves were blocking his field of vision, and she looked right at him. To her disappointment, his eyes moved over her without the slightest show of emotion, either approval or disapproval. But he *had* been looking for her because, once satisfied that he could recognize her whatever she got up to, he turned back to Lady Orsett, who was attired as Heaven-knew-what fantasy in ropes of pearls and quantities of insecure aigrette plumes.

Belle thoroughly enjoyed herself. She loved dancing and the simplicity of her costume made it far more of a pleasure for her than for many of the others who had aimed solely at effect. The food and wine, as usual, were sumptuous and she was delighted by the dozen flirtations which were going on around her and indulged in a few herself. She danced with Hugo, who held her closely but seemed abstracted and had little to say—perhaps because she unwisely sang Muriella's praises and stressed her good nature, her competence and her vibrant personality. She then faced the horror of dancing with Mr. Goldspink, who wasn't very good but was enthusiastic and grateful.

"Mask or no mask, I know who you are and, believe me, Miss Barclay, it is a very great honor for me to be dancing with you. I've always been stagestruck."

"You have theatrical connections?" enquired Belle, recalling Lawton's confidences.

"On the business side," replied Goldspink. "*Mrs.* Goldspink wouldn't give the go-ahead to my having connections of any kind with lovely young actresses, I can tell you!"

He squeezed her, and disconcertingly missed some steps.

"No sir," he chuckled. "Mrs. Goldspink would *not.*"
He seemed inordinately pleased about this.

"She's watching us now," he commented, and Belle glanced across the room to meet the suspicious stare of Mrs. Goldspink, tricked out as a Roman matron, looking quite prepared to fall on somebody's sword or something equally disagreeable. She was in the arms of a perspiring matador.

"Mrs. Goldspink's not in the best of humors tonight," confided Mr. Goldspink. "Muriella has gotten the bit between her teeth and defied her in the matter of her fancy dress."

"I think she looks lovely," remarked Belle, "and Lord Orsett has been paying her marked attention."

"He danced with her once," said Mr. Goldspink. "Duty dance."

"Well, he looked as if the duty were a pleasure," pursued Belle.

"My little girl doesn't stand a chance with you around, Miss Barclay," said Mr. Goldspink sadly. "She can make sheep's eyes and her mother can talk big and the Colonel can throw out orders, but she doesn't stand a chance. No sir, not a chance."

Belle said nothing, but she started thinking.

"Well, well," continued Mr. Goldspink, coming out of a dream, "what's Lawton's next venture to be, Miss Barclay? When shall I have the pleasure of attending the Diadem again on eighteen consecutive nights especially to see you?"

He was pressing rather closer than Belle found agreeable. Neither would the Roman matron have appreciated it, had she not been too occupied in reversing. Belle had a few seconds in which to make a momentous decision. She commended her future to the Fates and made it.

"You won't, Mr. Goldspink. Lawton has turned me off."

Mr. Goldspink was appalled and stopped dancing altogether.

"You mean—you can't mean—your theatrical career is finished? That I cannot believe."

"A little difference of opinion," remarked Belle easily. "It's time I had a change. I was wondering what the chances were in the States."

"In the States," repeated Goldspink, not seeming to comprehend, but starting to shuffle round again.

"It's a choice between trying my luck abroad, and marrying," Belle told him very deliberately.

"Going abroad or marrying," repeated Goldspink.

"Yes, either is a gamble. What do you think, Mr. Goldspink?"

"What do I think?"

Good God! Had she to spell it out for him?

"As you have theatrical interests in America, Mr. Goldspink, I thought you might be able to give me an introduction. If not, I think I shall marry. Perhaps that would be best anyway," she ended briskly as if tired of the subject. "Oh, the dance has ended, and it's midnight so we must unmask. There! Well, there were no surprises, were there? And here comes Mr. Arbuthnot, who has the next dance."

But Mr. Goldspink, still masked, was staring at her, oblivious of all else.

"I can say nothing now, Miss Barclay," he whispered. "But do not act hastily. I cannot allow such a loss to the profession, and I think—I *think*. . . . But do nothing hastily."

A good evening's work, decided Belle, as she allowed Tubby Arbuthnot to lead her away. She had swapped Hugo for a contract in America, for she had no doubt that Goldspink would get her one in exchange for a clear field for his only chick. The fact that Hugo wasn't hers to swap

was neither here nor there. At last things were beginning
to pick up, but her self-congratulations were short-lived.

"We've decided to stage something tonight, Miss Barclay, if that's all right by you," mouthed Tubby in her ear,
and Belle—she did not know why—abruptly stopped enjoying herself.

"The old man's been doing the pleasant," continued
Tubby, "handing out ices and compliments all evening.
Even danced a couple of times." Indeed, Belle had seen
the Colonel barking at various elderly nervous ladies and
being ferociously amiable to several tongue-tied young
ones. "But he sneaked out a few minutes back for a quiet
smoke in the shrubbery. So now's our chance for your
big love scene just so he can't possibly mistake the lie of
the land, don't you know. Hugo's waiting in the orangery.
Come on! Lord, Miss Barclay, I don't know when I've
laughed so much!"

Belle managed a weak smile.

"Don't worry, Miss Barclay. We shall be close behind
you. The old man won't make a scene in front of us and
we'll get you away safely, never fear."

The music crashed to a close. What the waltz was,
Belle had no idea, but she was glad it was good and loud
and that they had moved at a tremendous rate; Tubby
Arbuthnot's voice was hardly that of the perfect conspira-
tor. Shaking off old Mr. Arbuthnot, who had appeared
from nowhere, aghast at his son's companion, they made
their way to the orangery where Hugo was waiting.

"Still in the shrubbery, according to Ted," he reported.
"Give us ten minutes start."

Tubby thoughtfully produced a light silk wrap for Belle,
pronounced that the coast was clear and that Studholme
was on guard over Mother Sweeting, and Hugo and Belle
set off across the lawn towards the shrubbery. The moonlight made a pathway for them as they stole along, both

unconscious that they might have been ghosts from another century.

"We follow this path," said Hugo softly as they reached the spinney. "Walk slowly. I'll put my arm 'round you and you lean your head on my shoulder. There." They started along a winding, moonlight-dappled path.

"What a beastly place to come out to, to smoke," whispered Belle fretfully.

"Oh, he's an odd bird, the Colonel. He likes morbid, deserted places." Then his grip tightened. "I can see a cigar glowing slightly to the right." Belle could just make out the words. "I remember there's a seat over there where he sometimes rests. He must have seen us by now. Your white dress and wrap would show up against the trees and he's got eyes like a hawk. Would have heard our footsteps too. Just a few yards further and we shall be practically on top of him. Ready?"

Belle could hear his heart pounding and could feel herself shaking from top to toe. Stage fright, she told herself. Deep breaths! But, just as she was taking herself in hand, something *awful,* something eerie and spine-chilling circled close round their heads emitting shrill, high-pitched noises, and the brave Belle Barclay flung herself into Hugo's arms sobbing in terror, "Oh Hugo! *Bats!*" Instantly Hugo's arms closed around her, and a series of inexpert kisses poured down on Belle's ears and neck.

"Bats, Hugo," whimpered Belle into the painful gold braid. "I'm t-terrified of them!"

But Hugo's voice, now thick and hoarse, merely muttered, "Belle, I adore you, do you hear? I adore you. I can't let you go. I can't. You've got to marry me. I can't live without you. Oh, my darling! Say you love me. Say you're not playing with me."

And Belle, like the good trouper she was, came in on cue. "No, Hugo, I'm not playing. I love you, too. Oh darling!"

Their lips met in a long kiss which wasn't too bad really, she considered, by Hugo's standards. They seemed to stand there for an age, Belle with her eyes closed in apparent ecstasy and her ears strained to the utmost. Don't say the old blighter wasn't going to take any notice!

But eventually: "Well, well!" rasped an unpleasant voice, and Belle practically fainted with relief. She tore herself away from Hugo, losing her wrap as she did so, and confronted the Colonel with what she congratulated herself was a very creditable display of eye flashing and bosom heaving. *"You!"* she spat. "You were *spying* on us!"

The Colonel surveyed her coolly, still drawing on his cigar, then turned to Hugo, who put his arm round Belle again and pulled her close to him.

"Well sir!" said the Colonel. "What have you to say for yourself? Making love to a woman old enough to be your mother! A chorus girl twice your age!"

Belle quivered with rage, this time in earnest.

"I'm sorry if you don't approve, Uncle," said Hugo quietly. "But I love Miss Barclay and Miss Barclay loves me. She is going to honor me by becoming my wife. As that is so I cannot allow you to make any more vicious and untrue remarks about her or I shall be obliged to forget our relationship and call you out."

"Good God Almighty!" cried the Colonel, and dropped his cigar. "Do you mean, you young puppy, you intend to challenge me to a duel?"

"If necessary, sir, yes."

Hugo was shaking violently, and Belle blessed the darkness, for the moon had providentially gone behind a cloud. She was having a hard time keeping a straight face herself, even while still in terror that another bat might swoop down on her.

"Good God!" reiterated the Colonel. He seemed unable to take it in. "Well, I won't have it, d'you hear?"

he suddenly roared. "You're not marrying this tart, she'd make your life a perfect hell and drag you down to her own gutter level. You'd better explain to her the terms of your father's will and make it quite clear to her, or to her attorney, that you will be practically penniless if you marry without my blessing before you are twenty-five. She won't hang around you without Orsett Park and your fine horses and carriages and the family jewels, and your regiment, of course. You'll have to give that up."

Hugo gave the most authentic heartbroken gasp that Belle had ever heard, but he said, "Very well, sir. I shall find some means of livelihood. It will only be for four years."

"Last week it was that Sweeting female, now *this*. You don't know your own mind two minutes together, except that you are determined to make as unsuitable an alliance as you can. Julia Sweeting is a fool. This woman is an adventuress."

"Adventuress!" exploded Hugo.

"Adventuress," repeated the Colonel. "She has no intention of living in penury for four years, or for four months. She's using you for her own ends. What she wants to do is to extract money from me. To be bought off. It's quite a common occurrence."

"That's not true!" shouted Hugo.

"You leave her with me," suggested the Colonel, "and you'll find I'm right."

"I will not leave Miss Barclay with you!"

"Nonsense. You'll find we understand each other perfectly," retorted the Colonel. "It's not the first time I've done this sort of thing for other stupid young fellows. Ah, here come your friends looking for you. This way, gentlemen. Come, madam, we will stroll a little further."

Before Hugo could do anything, he was surrounded by his vociferous cronies, led by Tubby Arbuthnot, who made repellent noises and roared out that where Miss Barclay was, there would Hugo be. "Didn't I say so, Studholme? Why didn't you take me on?"

"I wasn't losing my money on a certainty," laughed Captain Studholme. "Not such a fool. Oh, evening, sir. Enjoying the dance? We're having a terrific time, but Miss Barclay and Hugo are missing all the fun. We've come to take them back."

"Take Hugo, by all means," entreated the Colonel. "He should not be neglecting his guests. I will escort Miss Barclay back to the house in a few minutes."

He had somehow deftly detached Belle from Hugo and now, placing her hand on his arm, he walked away with her. Although sorry for Hugo, Belle was overjoyed that her sole motive in coming was so well understood, and made not the slightest protest. As they went, she looked over her shoulder and could see his friends practically carrying the protesting Hugo away, although Tubby Arbuthnot was looking after her and the Colonel, plainly disturbed at this turn of events. *Ah well,* sauve qui peut, she thought, stepping out lightheartedly beside the Colonel. She just reached his shoulder which, for some reason, was rather nice. And she wouldn't have to go to America! *All in all,* Belle told herself, *we carried that off pretty well.*

"All in all," said the Colonel, "I flatter myself that we carried that off pretty well. Pretty well!"

8

Carried it off pretty well! Oh no! A little prickle of dread ran up and down Belle's spine. She had a horrible feeling that this was where the best-laid plans of Belle Barclay went quite agley.

"What do you mean?" she asked carefully.

"I never imagined that I would be called upon to play the 'heavy,' as I believe it is called, in an act from a *bona fide* musical comedy," replied the Colonel. "At least, that's what it sounded like to me. I never heard such trash in all my life. Thank God it's over. That's one blessing. I was far from keen on dragging the farce out until the end of the week. A shame you will be unable to stay for the birthday celebrations. You will leave today, I suppose? There's a good train back to town at ten-eight, or one just after four A.M., come to think of it. After all, there's nothing to keep you."

She should never have consented to this evening's farago. Never! Not with the Goldspink approach at such a delicate point of balance. She must have been mad! She should have insisted on waiting a few more days before taking on the Colonel. Now she had lost everything. *Fool! Fool! Fool!*

"Indeed? Why should I go back to town?" Belle heard herself demanding. "Lady Orsett has invited me for the week."

"Ye-es, Lady Orsett," repeated the Colonel in a faraway voice which boded no good for that lady. "You will leave in the morning, if you have any sense, because the game is up. My nephew is not going to marry you. He does not want to marry you. He wouldn't marry you if you were served up on a golden salver with parsley. He wants to marry Julia Sweeting. This pathetic plan, if plan it can be called, of bringing you here to frighten me into insisting that he marry Miss Sweeting, is so fantastic that it could only have originated in the brain of that prize fool, Peregrine Arbuthnot. As I know the threat to be totally idle on Hugo's part and as I have no intention of buying you off with so much as a sovereign, as you had hoped, you have all failed dismally and some other means must be found of gaining my consent. In the meantime, you are of no further use to Hugo and will, in fact, be an embarrassment."

Belle could do nothing but play the scene out to the bitter end. She fell back on *The Naiad and the Nabob*. "You are mistaken, Colonel Gore," she retorted. "Your nephew is in love with me and I with him. With or without your consent we intend to marry."

"And trust to my relenting when the heir arrives a year later?"

At the near-repetition of her own words to Hugo, Belle blushed crimson.

"You might *just* manage it," said the Colonel, looking at her critically.

Belle smacked his face.

The Colonel made no move to show that he had noticed, but merely replaced her hand on his arm and continued walking. "You see, Miss Barclay," he said in an almost pleading way, "I have been vastly entertained by you on many occasions. I quite enjoyed our little scene just now. I have always admired you and I still admire you. If I didn't, you would have had your marching orders two minutes after I first saw you here, when you were brought in to tea by that Yankee you had already captivated just by walking down the stairs with him. I don't blame him. You looked bewitching. You always look bewitching. I decided then to let you play out your little part, whatever it was. I hope Hugo has paid your expenses, because I won't. There is no danger of Hugo marrying you rather than Miss Sweeting."

"And *if* there were?" asked Belle, talking for the sake of it.

"Good God! I should prefer him to marry you rather than that nitwit," said the Colonel, surprisingly. Belle nearly collapsed.

"I wouldn't give my consent, naturally," continued the Colonel, "because you have no fortune and Orsett Park must have a fortune. It's Orsett Park that's marrying, not Hugo. But, if it came to it, I would rather he married you than Miss Sweeting. So, you see, Arbuthnot's plot was doomed from the start. It rested upon an entirely false premise."

Belle was digesting this when—squeak! squeak!—and the tiniest bat in the world flew harmlessly past. It was enough for Belle. She was instantly buried in the Colonel's arms, sobbing hysterically, "Don't let it come near me! It will get into my hair!"

"As if I would let the brute get into its beautiful hair then!" soothed the Colonel tenderly, his hard fingers running through her disheveled curls. "What a stupid idiot it is!"—and he kissed the tip of her nose and then each eye and then her mouth, once at each corner and once in the middle.

"Has it gone?" trembled Belle.

"Yes, but I haven't," said the Colonel.

Captain Studholme was right. The Colonel had been the rounds. He was an expert. After a token struggle, Belle surrendered to his kisses, caresses and outrageous murmured endearments and let herself forget everything else. This would be a precious memory when she was an old lady eking out a precarious existence, probably selling gin in some Wapping back alley. Then as the Colonel abandoned kissing her mouth in favor of her throat and shoulders, and seemed disposed to continue on his downward path, saner thoughts prevailed. Why should she, Isabelle Mary Barclay, allow herself to give a few minutes' diversion to a man who had ordered her off the premises, who had jeered at her age and, not content with that, put several years on to it, who had called her a tart and an ageing chorus girl? Her blood was up!

"You have refused to buy me off, Colonel Gore," she said sweetly, "but will you be paying me for this?"

The Colonel had one last leisurely kiss and then looked at her with dark, unfathomable eyes which gradually became contemptuous.

"I am afraid I expect rather more if money is to change hands," he drawled, "but if you wish I am sure we can come to some amicable pecuniary arrangement. I had no idea your finances were so pressing. Forgive me. Shall I come to your room? Or would you prefer to return to Orsett Court with me? Your maid no doubt knows how to cope when you are absent for the night."

At least he had learned his lesson and wasn't going to repeat the face slapping. One hand held both Belle's wrists pinioned behind her back.

"You—you *beast!*" sobbed Belle, really struggling now. "Let me go!"

"Certainly," said the Colonel, releasing her at once, but keeping a wary eye on her. "By the way, it has been raining steadily for some time. We have been slightly sheltered but you will get decidedly wet returning to the house. You had better wait here and let me send someone with a waterproof."

"I don't care if I *drown!*" screamed Belle, and snatching up her crumpled and bedraggled wrap and draping it around her as best she could, she ran towards the house with rain and tears cascading down her face. Flying in at a side entrance, she careered straight into the arms of Hugo! *Oh no,* thought Belle, *not another of them!* But Hugo held on to her and kissed her wet face and demanded, "Belle, my darling, I've been out of my mind. Those fools dragged me back here by force. I shall never forgive my uncle for what he said to you. Never. I got away as soon as I could and I've been searching the house. I thought he must have brought you back long ago. It's pouring! How could he have kept you out there?"

"It was sheltered where we were," gulped Belle.

"Then why didn't he leave you there and come back for a waterproof for you?" demanded Hugo, looking thunderous. "What was he thinking of? In that stupid thin muslin, you're frozen. You'll get a chill."

"He offered to but I wouldn't let him. Let me go, Hugo. I'll have a hot bath and go to bed. Has the party broken up?"

"Just about. Oh, darling, kiss me!"

"It's no use, Hugo, he saw through the whole plot. Even guessed whose idea it was. He's called your bluff. Says he knows very well you would never marry me, and what could I say to that? I tried my best, but it was no good. I'm sorry."

Hugo stared at her. "Belle, dearest, are you all right? Of course I'm going to marry you! I told you so, don't you remember, my love? And you said that you loved me. Belle, you've made me the happiest man on earth!"

It was Belle's turn to stare. "You mean—you *meant* it?" she croaked.

"Of course I meant it," cried Hugo, hugging her even closer. "Oh, stupid, stupid Belle! How many times do I have to tell you? I'm in love with you. I think I always have been, right from the first time I saw you at the Diadem, but when you came into my arms tonight like that—well, I just knew."

"But the plan?" said Belle, wildly. "Tubby Arbuthnot's plan?"

"Tubby Arbuthnot!" said Hugo venemously. "I knocked Tubby Arbuthnot down half an hour ago. I've had enough of him and his plans. I'm going to marry you Belle. I adore you. I can't live without you." And once again Belle was held in desperate arms and kissed until her head reeled.

"Hugo, if you don't let me go, I think I shall go mad," she managed to say at last. "Somebody will come along and see us."

"I want everyone to see us," said Hugo grandly.

By some feat of strength which Belle hadn't imagined herself capable of, she got out of his clutches and dashed up the nearest stairs, Hugo keeping pace effortlessly beside her. She stopped on the first landing and obediently Hugo stopped too. She dragged the soaking wet wrap round her shoulders, shook the wet curls out of her eyes and tried again.

"Now look," she said. "I never dreamed that you were doing anything but play-acting. It was all I was doing. I don't love you and couldn't possibly marry you and when you've calmed down—for I think you must have been drinking far too heavily this evening—you will realize how impossible the whole thing is. Anyway, your uncle has told me I must leave by the ten-eight."

She instantly regretted that remark, for Hugo went scarlet. "How *dare* he! I shall go and see him at once. I shall—"

"Please! Hugo!"

"Say you won't leave then. Promise me faithfully."

He caught her wrist in a steel grip and looked frightening. Her expressive face must have depicted her sudden fear, for he relaxed his grip and became the old Hugo again, but there was some quality there, Belle realized, that she had never glimpsed before or suspected. Something which would come out strongly when he was older. Good heavens! He might even get like the Colonel!

"Promise then," said Hugo. "I must see you tomorrow. Early. Come riding with me before we have to go on that blasted expedition. Meet me at the stables at nine. You do ride?"

"Yes, but I haven't a habit."

"I'll get Bridgers to find you one," said Hugo. "Promise me on your honor that you'll come, otherwise I shall stand outside your bedroom door all night to see you don't sneak off."

As they had then reached her bedroom door and there was nothing in the world Belle wanted more than to get behind it, and as he was perfectly capable of carrying out his threat, Belle promised. At that moment, the door opened and Daisy peeped out. Her eye took in instantly the soaked muslin, which was clinging to Belle like a second skin.

"Until tomorrow morning then," said Hugo, and with one last lingering kiss, he walked away down the corridor.

"What's up?" snapped Daisy.

"Just get my bath and get me to bed," said Belle. "The Colonel's rumbled the whole thing."

Daisy's mouth opened to form the words: *I told you so.*

"Oh no, you didn't and, what's more, he hasn't!" cut in Belle savagely. "There's nothing to rumble. Hugo really has fallen in love with me and we're in the very devil of a mess. Don't say another word about it, Daisy, I can't stand any more!"

And Daisy, good old Daisy, didn't!

9

Morning came bright and clear, and etched against it was Daisy, sharp and black and in a bad temper. She was holding a riding habit.

"Her Ladyship's maid gave me this for you. She thinks it will fit. She said you was going riding with His Lordship at nine, so I thought I'd better wake you early or *I'd* get the blame. You never told me."

Her tone plainly implied that there was a lot more Belle hadn't told her, too, but Belle was in no mood for confidences and a reproachful silence fell. Belle looked splendid in the dark riding habit, with her shining gold hair pinned up neatly in coils and showing off the lovely bone structure of her face. *Looks something like a marchioness or countess,* thought Daisy, *much more than the old baggages we got here.* She wouldn't have said so for worlds. She was cross with Belle and hurt too. She wanted to know what had happened last night but Belle volunteered no further information, which wasn't like Belle. Something had happened to really shake Belle, something more than his lordship's sudden proposal, of that Daisy was certain. The servants' hall reported that her mistress and his lordship had gone out together in the grounds. He had come back first with a crowd of his friends. She had run in, soaked to the skin, a long time later. Why? He had been waiting for her and had kissed her shamelessly time and again—and her like that!— on their way up to her room, but he hadn't gone in.

"He certainly did not!" said Daisy. "I was there and there was nothing of that!"

Well, what was it all about then, the stewards' room and Servants' Hall wanted to know. Although no one said so, they obviously all believed that Daisy knew more than she was saying. The fact that she didn't, but she ought to have done, was driving her wild. She cleared up Belle's dressing table in a fury, while Belle herself trailed down to breakfast.

The Marchioness was in the dining room, helping herself to kidney from the sideboard, when Belle entered. Most of the gentlemen were there, including Hugo's friends, all in an agitated state. Tubby Arbuthnot had a black eye, and old Mr. Arbuthnot was beside himself. "Retire to your room, I beg you, Peregrine! An eye specialist must be sought. I must speak to Colonel Gore. The sight may be irretrievably impaired."

"Mornin', Miss Barclay. Going ridin'?" asked Captain Studholme nervously.

Belle nodded and waded in to the bacon and eggs.

"Miss Barclay has a good appetite," observed the Marquis, shuddering at the food and pouring himself a drink.

"One should eat heartily while one has the chance," the Marchioness told him tartly.

A good shot, considered Belle. Much nearer than the old girl knew.

"Piranti won the race, I hear," remarked another man hastily, with a masculine dread of scenes. "Came down near Tours in the early hours. Nobody else got as far as that. Cable came for Hugo. Fotheringay opened it. Suppose Hugo knows, but he didn't seem interested, I thought. Funny, he was obsessed with balloons at the beginning of the year."

The Marchioness sighed. Belle sneezed.

"It rained hard last night," said several people at once, and immediately wished they hadn't.

"You're coming on the expedition, aren't you, Miss Barclay? Hugo will be there. I m-m-mean—" stammered a youngster.

"We all know what you mean, Edward," said the Marchioness in the silence which followed.

Belle finished her coffee, gave the assembled company one of her slow, sleepy smiles, and went down to the stables. Hugo, looking older and handsomer and much more sure of himself than she had ever seen him, was talking to a groom. Two horses had been led out, the smaller chestnut evidently being hers. As Hugo came to meet her, Belle saw that he had grown up overnight. He *was* in love with her. Nobody could possibly mistake the way he looked at her. He didn't speak but, despite the groom's presence, he kissed her lightly on the lips, then he swung her up bodily on to the chestnut.

Belle had loved riding as a child, but it was years since she had been able to indulge in it, and she never had sat such a sweet little thoroughbred as she did now. Hugo blessedly said nothing as they let their horses have their heads over the short springy turf. The world was fresh and new after its wash. When they eventually drew rein beside the river, Belle was flushed and laughing, and Hugo leaned over and kissed her.

"Good morning, Miss Barclay," he said. "When will you marry me?"

"Hugo, you ridiculous boy!" laughed Belle, determined to keep it light. "You know your uncle has seen through it and you'll just have to think up some other way. I'm going to enjoy the rest of my week and you're not to spoil it!"

Hugo did not, as she had thought he would, get red and belligerent. He remained quiet and older—oh, so much older—and Belle didn't like it.

"After the childish way in which I've behaved, I'm not surprised that you shouldn't believe me. But you'll have to, my darling. You'll have to!"

Belle thought he was going to kiss her again but their horses chose that moment to get excited and restive. A few moments later the reason became apparent. The Colonel and another man were riding towards them; the Colonel, naturally enough, thought Belle, on an enormous coal-black beast which was probably a battle-scarred, seasoned campaigner itself.

"Don't quarrel with him Hugo, please," she begged in an undertone.

"In front of Fotheringay?" said Hugo distastefully.

"Good morning, Miss Barclay. Good morning, Hugo," the Colonel called out, and Fotheringay touched his cap with his riding crop and swelled with excitement. His lordship and the playactress riding alone! This would be something to tell the stewards' room and Mrs. Fotheringay!

"An elm's fallen across the bridleway down by Little Bishops," reported the Colonel. "Hasn't done Jessop's cottage much good, but could have been worse. At least no one was injured. Fotheringay's getting it cut up today and some temporary repairs to Jessop's place put in hand. A good opportunity, Hugo, to have some radical improvements done there. It's the worst cottage on the estate.

Didn't realize how bad it was until I went in just now. A hovel!"

"Waste of money sir," put in Fotheringay ingratiatingly. "Mrs. J is a filthy trollop."

"If she'd got something better to live in, it might give her some self-respect," said the Colonel. "I'll go and put the fear of God into her myself, and into Jessop. He's a decent enough fellow, but too easy with her, I fancy. These good-looking women get far too much latitude."

His eyes met Belle's briefly.

"Wants to take a stick to her, eh, sir?" leered Fotheringay.

The Colonel ignored him. "All those elms ought to come down, Hugo. They're damned treacherous trees."

"Oh no! They're beautiful!" cried Belle involuntarily, and indeed the great trees serene and English against the heat haze were magnificent.

"Quite so!" sneered the Colonel, his eyes again just meeting Belle's. "Many beautiful things are more trouble than they're worth. However, I shall leave that decision to Hugo—that is, if he is interested in such mundane and unromantic matters as the running of his estate," he added meaningfully.

Or if Hugo is still in a position to be consulted, thought Belle. Hugo evidently thought so too, because he made no comment although he looked at the distant elms as if he were seeing them for the first time. Then he looked back at Belle, and his face cleared as if by magic.

"Race you back," he challenged. "I'll give you half a minute's start!"

"You'll need more than half a minute, Miss Barclay," joked Fotheringay, "more than half a minute to escape His Lordship when he's after you!"

Both the Colonel and Hugo turned identical looks of freezing disdain on Fotheringay, who backed away and muttered something about getting the men up to Jessops.

"As quickly as you wish, Fotheringay," said the Colonel nastily.

"Are you coming on the expedition to the Abbey, Uncle?" asked Hugo.

"I suppose so. Of all the tedious wastes of time! I shall be remarkably glad, Hugo, when this week is over."

He gave Belle a glance of dislike, which she was expecting, and which she parried with a brilliant smile. She had the joy of seeing the Colonel momentarily disconcerted.

"Well, I must return to the Court," he muttered. "Wait for me, Fotheringay!"

"How's the Parliamentary business going?" asked Hugo.

"Oh all right," grunted the Colonel who, curiously, now seemed to be the one who was ill at ease. "I'll see you later. Good morning, Miss Barclay."

Hugo and Belle turned their horses back towards the Park and rode along companionably. How odd to have been holding quite an ordinary conversation about elm trees and hovels with two men both of whom, a few hours previously, had been doing their best to kiss her senseless, thought Belle. It was while puzzling over this that she saw Julia Sweeting, appropriately mounted on a nursery-rhyme dapple-gray, cantering towards them.

"Here's Miss Sweeting," she remarked. "I say—she's crying!"

"Oh Lord!" muttered Hugo, after a sheepish glance. "Quick, Belle! You'd better go!"

But there was no time. Julia was there. Besides, Belle was curious.

"Oh, Hugo," sobbed Julia. "You p-pwomised to mawwy me. You p-p-womised. When we were widing on the haycart and you cut off one of my winglets and took it back to school with you and the headmaster found it and beat you! And now you have written me a b-b-beastly letter, all stiff and cold, and said you *won't*! And you pwomised me! And my m-m-mama did too! That I should be a countess and live at Orsett Park, and now she is cwoss and she says it is all my fault for being so slow!"

"As I explained in my letter, Julia," Hugo said, "those promises were made when I was very much underage. In fact, as you yourself have just pointed out, while I was still a schoolboy and in no position to promise anything, and although I deeply regret any pain I have caused you I am afraid that I now agree with my uncle that a marriage between us would be unsuitable. I hope we shall always be friends but there is nothing more to say. Come, Belle!" And Hugo rode off, thankfully, Belle guessed.

"My mama says it's all your fault!" accused Julia, poking Belle with her riding crop.

"Well, she can't have it both ways," objected Belle. "It can't be all your fault *and* all mine as well. She will have to apportion it."

This had the effect of making Julia cry harder than ever.

"I'm not clever like you," she hiccupped. "That's why Hugo won't mawwy me!"

"Dry your eyes, Miss Sweeting, and tell me exactly what has happened," ordered Belle.

"I had a letter fwom Hugo this morning," sniffed Julia. "My mama opened it of course and wead it and went into hystewwics! I had to give her sal volatile," she recalled proudly. "Hugo said his uncle would never consent and that it wasn't fair to hold me to any boy-and-girl pwomises when he had no pwospects, and I'm so unhappy!" bawled Julia.

Belle couldn't feel that Julia's grief was very deep, but undoubtedly the girl would be in for a time of it at her mother's hands for having let such a prize slip.

"And what did your mama say? About me?"

"She said it was all your doing. She said you were determined to get him, and get him you would, whatever
the Colonel said. She said Hugo was only making
thweadbare excuses."

Another cascade of tears. Belle ignored Hugo's calls
and said calmly, "But he wasn't making excuses, you
know. Lord Orsett was merely stating an undeniable
fact. His uncle will not give his consent to your marriage."

"I know," cried Julia, "but I don't know why he
shouldn't. He's always quite nice to me, although he's a
bit gwuff."

"I know why," said Belle. "He's in love with you himself!"

What devil had prompted her to say such a thing, she
didn't know, but she was amazed at the effect. Julia's
tears dried magically.

"*Colonel Gore!*" she breathed. "In love with me? But
he's an *old* man!"

Much you know, thought Belle. *Five minutes with him,
my girl, and you'd be feeling like a rag doll.* However,
Julia had already dismissed the idea herself.

"Well, he's *oldish,*" Julia conceded. "But he's a vewwy
bwave man. He won the V.C. For killing people." Before
Belle's eyes, Julia recovered like a violet after a thunder-
storm. "Oh, thank you, Miss Barclay. Thank you! I never
dweamed! Colonel Gore! I think he looks older than he is.
Colonel Gore!"

"You're coming on the expedition?" asked Belle, as she
turned her horse away, well satisfied with her morning's
work.

"Oh yes!" breathed Julia rapturously. "I shall sit with
Colonel Gore!"

And serve him right, thought Belle, as she galloped off
to join a furiously impatient Hugo.

"Belle! Why on earth were you encouraging that
wretched girl? I'm doing my best to shake her off and you
sit there half an hour talking to her!"

So much for last week's undying love, thought Belle wryly.

"Oh, cheering her up," she said vaguely. "She's coming on the picnic anyway."

Hugo groaned. "The Sweetings would come anywhere. They'll be at the Park tonight and the shoot tomorrow. By the way, sweetheart, are you coming?"

Belle's shudder was eloquent.

Hugo laughed but his eyes were adoring. "No, you're too soft and gentle for that, aren't you, dearest? Oh Belle, you are the most divine—"

"Have they been invited to the Colonel's dinner party?" interrupted Belle.

"Yes, they'll be there. And at everything on my birthday too."

"Well, everybody's going to be there," said Belle. "The Princesses, and some old duchess of ninety, whoever she may be."

"Some old duchess! That's my grandmother! The Duchess of Peckham. Uncle Piers's mother."

Belle nearly fell off her horse.

"Didn't you think he'd have a mother?" laughed Hugo. "She's a queer old bird. Rows with everyone. Quite a girl in her youth. Her father was a wealthy ironmonger in the north. Name of Shoveller. Caused a scandal when she married my grandfather. When he died, she upped and married the Duke of Peckham, who was a widower and about a hundred and fifty. She turned him off after a few months."

"And she presented an organ to the church here in memory of your grandfather at a cost of £500 in 1884," said Belle.

"That's right," agreed Hugo, abstractedly, to Belle's chagrin not finding it odd that she should have such a piece of information at her fingertips.

Belle was totally uninterested in the twice-married,

nonagenarian, antagonistic Duchess of Peckham, but at least the Duchess had diverted Hugo's attention sufficiently for them to reach the stables without having to endure any more of Hugo's extravagant twaddle. There he was immediately buttonholed by the head groom and Belle slipped away and strolled back to the house alone, where she found the expedition to the Abbey getting under way. Tubby Arbuthnot and Captain Studholme were carrying a hamper out to load into a wagonette.

"Just giving a hand with the booze," explained Tubby. His eye was distinctly off-color, but he seemed to bear no ill will. "I say, Miss Barclay, what *did* happen last night? Old Hugo was in the devil of a bate and we can't get a thing out of him. Got quite nasty with me, in fact."

"Ran into the Colonel earlier on," said Captain Studholme, "and he cut me dead."

"The scene went ahead as planned," said Belle, "was witnessed by Colonel Gore, and totally disbelieved." The two young men groaned. "You should have got somebody younger and prettier," continued Belle.

But both protested vigorously. "What did he *say?*" worried Captain Studholme.

"Nothing much," said Belle. "We got caught in the rain."

"My man told me you ran in soaked to the skin," said Tubby, "and that Hugo—you know how they talk in the servants' hall, but the damned thing is they're usually right—Hugo has asked you to marry him in earnest. And the betting is that you will. It's a dead cert. Sledgeman's closed his book. I never even got a sovereign on," he complained, "and I'm Hugo's best friend!"

"I'm sorry," said Belle, nettled. "I did my best, but it's all over. As for this other nonsense, words fail me! Now I must go and change."

"Oh good! You're coming on the picnic?" said Captain Studholme.

"Yes, with Hugo," replied Belle and left them to work that one out.

The dreamlike day slowly unrolled, if a dream in brilliant sunshine is feasible. It remained for Belle a time of isolated scenes, each one perfect in its timing and coloring and effect. The cool green marble of the river as she and Hugo drifted down between banks of giant kingcups, the cattle kneedeep in the lush grass. The ruined abbey, its days of turmoil done, deserted and peaceful, sheep cropping round it. The *al fresco* luncheon. The women looking divine in their pastel voiles, their faces shaded by the silken fringes of their parasols, the men like gods, except for Mr. Arbuthnot and Mr. Goldspink, who wore a ridiculous floppy hat and perspired a great deal.

She saw an entrancing Julia Sweeting being helped from his boat by the Colonel. She saw the Marquis raise a brandy bottle and the Marchioness raise her lorgnette. She saw the Colonel handing Julia her sketching pad and settling her down with a great quantity of cushions in the shade. She saw Mr. Goldspink taking photographs, and she even consented to pose for him in the ruined nave amongst the sheep, and against splendid archways leading nowhere. Goldspink was in ecstasies and murmured in her ear, "Do nothing yet, Miss Barclay, do nothing yet. I may soon have news," before being called to his wife's side. She saw the Colonel helping Julia to cold chicken. She saw Mrs. Sweeting looking very, very thoughtful. She saw Muriella in strident green with violet ribbons, circulating amongst the groups and talking and laughing animatedly. She saw the Countess ineffectually swatting a wasp. She saw Tubby Arbuthnot in the classic position of being left clinging to his punt pole in the middle of the river while the punt drifted slowly on and old Mr. Arbuthnot wailed, "Peregrine! My boy!" from the bank.

And through it all, Mrs. Goldspink's loud, assertive voice went on and on.

They packed up and went home in the late afternoon. She changed into her diaphonous rose-pink for tea and then into her pearl satin with the innumerable tiny buttons for dinner and for strolling in the grounds with Hugo, while a hidden orchestra played Mozart, Haydn and Strauss, and Tettrazini sang in the orangery, and Chinese lanterns festooned the trees and turned the Park into fairyland.

Belle was sitting on the terrace while Hugo had gone to get her an ice, idly watching knots of people come in, go out, form into groups, disburse and re-form, when she became aware of a breathless voice in her ear and a plump form nestling down beside her.

"It's still very warm," said the Countess, "and September tomorrow, too! I'm afraid I've hardly seen you since you arrived, Miss Barclay, but I'm so busy, you know!"

Belle smilingly agreed.

"I know all about—*it*," whispered the Countess, moving closer. "The others don't. Not the Marchioness, not even Bridgers. They keep trying to frighten me by telling me that you have set your cap at Hugo. They can't understand why I take it so calmly! They think it's because I'm a socialist, like Lady Warwick! 'Hugo may marry where he chooses,' I say. 'It's none of our concern.' But we know better, don't we?"

Poor soul, thought Belle, *she's several acts behind.* Evidently Hugo hadn't seen fit to bring his mother up to date on the latest turn of events.

"Such a nice little girl, Julia Sweeting," said the Countess, "and such a pity the Colonel so objects to her."

The Colonel chose that very moment to walk by with Julia, a sapphire chiffon vision, on his arm. "Good heavens!" exclaimed the startled Countess. "He's coming 'round! Well done, my dear! Well, well, who would have thought it? I really believe the Colonel is coming 'round!"

10

Next morning Belle was awakened by distant shots. It was the mystic First and the slaughter of the partridges had begun. Daisy was quietly moving about the room. She had already drawn back the curtains to reveal, for the first time of their stay, a gray day.

"Is it raining?" asked Belle cautiously.

"I'd call it rain but they call it a heavy dew," answered Daisy. "They've all gone off anyway in their tweeds and boots *and* they're welcome. That Marchioness has got on a hat I wouldn't give to the ragman. Do you want your breakfast?"

"Of course I want my breakfast. Off you go and see if anything's left."

There was plenty left and more than either of them had bargained for. Daisy came back, white-faced, with a laden tray and a letter.

"It's from *him!*" she gasped.

"Who?"

"The Colonel! His man just rode up with it and said it was to be given to you instanter. Oh Belle!"

It lay on the bed and they looked at it for a long time. After fortifying herself with coffee, porridge swimming in cream, hot rolls and honey, Belle took the thick, square, white envelope, from which her name in firm black handwriting stared up at her.

"Wait till His Lordship comes back," begged Daisy.

"Don't be such a fool! It's probably to say that he doesn't want me at his dinner party tonight. Or more likely it encloses a couple of railway tickets."

Savagely she tore the envelope open and unfolded the sheet of crackling paper.

> Orsett Court
>
> Madam,
>   I shall be obliged if you will favor me with a few minutes of your time this morning. I shall send a conveyance for you at eleven A.M. and trust this will be convenient.
>
>   Yours etc.,
>   P.H.L.L.Gore

"Oh, my Gawd!" was Daisy's instant and only-to-be-expected reaction.

"He's going to *give* me a couple of railway tickets then. Well, stir your stumps, Daisy. We haven't got much time."

"*We* haven't?"

"No, *we* haven't. I'm not going there alone. It's not proper. I wonder he dared suggest it."

"I'll come with you, but I can't come into his *room*," breathed Daisy. "Besides, he wouldn't have me. You're the one who's going to get it in the neck, not me."

"Why have I got to go there?" wondered Belle. "Why doesn't he come here? Anyway, why isn't he out shooting with the rest? Surely that would be just up his street, being exposed to heavy crossfire and all that."

"Nabbs—"

"Nabbs?"

Daisy went a bit pink. "His man. Nabbs said he was laid up with the gout."

"The *gout!* Heavens above! He'll be in a sweet temper then."

"We ought to try and get word to his lordship," worried Daisy. "He's trying to get rid of you before His Lordship gets back, mark my words."

"Don't be so melodramatic, Daisy. He's in a foul mood and I'm to stand in as whipping boy. Perhaps it's something to do with Julia Sweeting."

"What about her?" asked Daisy. "In the servants' hall they say that she's going all out for him. They said it was disgusting the way she followed him about yesterday and her mother *condoning* of it! She put the girl up to it, that's certain!"

Belle started to giggle. "No she didn't, *I* did. I told Julia that the Colonel objected to her marrying Hugo because he wanted her for himself!"

"What the 'ell did you do that for?" demanded Daisy, open-mouthed.

"Just to make mischief, I suppose."

"You must be out of your wits," whimpered Daisy, in a rising panic. "That fool of a girl has told him what you said and he's going to have you up on false pretenses. You'll land up in prison. I know it!"

Belle blissfully licked the last of the cream from her fingers and handed the depleted tray to Daisy. "I think that I had better look pretty," she decided. "Now, what will do that?"

The striped silver and blue broché and the saucy straw boater did it. Daisy, stiff and straight in her best black, was Virtue's Champion. Punctually at eleven A.M., the

Colonel's man arrived driving a neat little trap and they climbed aboard. Nabbs looked as if he had been chipped, painfully, out of granite. He did not speak but drove them at a good safe clip along the short distance which separated Orsett Park from Orsett Court.

A square brick mansion it was, as Kelly's *Directory* had noted, but Kelly should have gone further and said a *dismal* square brick mansion. The grounds appeared to be all that was claimed in size, although no deer antlered its way out to greet them. There was something about the place which made Belle sad. It couldn't be called neglected, but there was nothing to attract the eye. Orsett Park with its lake, its terrace, urns of tumbling fuchsias and geraniums, classical statuary, and striped blinds at all the windows, had spoiled Belle and Daisy for such austerity. The place was shrouded in a particularly dark, plain variety of ivy and the windows peered through it blankly. It was quiet and deserted, no servants bustling about, not even a canine equivalent of the Countess' pug dogs barking.

Nabbs handed them down and led them into a large, but dark and damp, hall.

"Wait here," he ground out.

"Chatty, isn't he?" said Belle. Her voice echoed.

" 'E can talk if 'e wants to. Just don't want to. Got the miseries this morning," sniffed Daisy.

"I should have the miseries every morning if I lived here. It's like a tomb. And look at that marvelous great fireplace. Just fancy that with a Yule Log burning!"

"They ought to have this *'ideous* carpet up. It's threadbare. No wonder my feet are perished."

"Yes, and they ought to clear out all this furniture. What is it anyway? A set of armories or something. Dark, depressing stuff. He need talk about Mrs. Jessop and her hovel!"

"And the dust," complained Daisy. "I could write my

name on this table." Removing her glove she traced SLUT in large letters on a table which held a bowl (which might have been silver) containing a few ancient visiting cards, a riding crop and two dead spiders. "That ought to shame somebody," she said, returning to her chair, "but it won't. He don't have anyone here but that Nabbs, he's his ex-batman, and a couple of the biggest trollops in the village, Mrs. Boosey and Eliza Mary Figgins, who's halfwitted as well. Mrs. Culpepper told me."

"But *why?* He's not hard up, surely?"

"No, they say he just don't worry."

"And yet he's such a good trustee to Hugo's estate. I suppose he's just not domesticated. *Daisy Sash!* He's got that dinner party tonight! No wonder none of the girls wanted to come! He just *can't!* Not in this mausoleum! We shall have to do something!"

They were staring at one another in desperation when Nabbs returned.

"The Colonel will see you now," he said to Belle. "You wait here," he ordered Daisy.

Daisy bridled, but whatever she may have been going to say was lost in Nabbs's roar of fury when he saw the table.

"Who did this?" he demanded. "Come on now, who did this?"

"I did," said Daisy belligerently. "So what?"

"I'll— I'll— I won't have it, that's what!" bellowed Nabbs. "Supposing the Colonel had seen it! What would he have said?"

"Why? Does he do the dusting?" inquired Daisy with interest.

"You—you interfering, meddling—"

"Look, Nabbs," interrupted Belle, "how are you managing this dinner party tonight?"

"The caterers are coming in," said Nabbs sullenly.

"But who is going to clear up?"

"What is necessary will be done," said Nabbs grandly. "I have served with the Colonel for twenty-five years and I hope I know my business."

"You shine his boots lovely," said Daisy, "but, let's face it, you'd never make a housemaid. Why don't you stir up them two lazy hussies you've got down there in your kitchen? But there," she added nastily, "perhaps they're kept as company for the pair of you. Perhaps they're too exhausted by their other duties." She looked meaningly at Belle.

"If you think the Colonel would soil his hands with either of them, you're out of your mind," whispered Nabbs, horror-struck. "I doubt if he knows they're in the house."

"No one would know they're in the house for what they do," said Daisy.

Without doubt, Daisy was getting in all the points and Nabbs knew it. Belle half-wondered if he was going to resort to violence but a sudden roar caused all three of them to leap to attention.

"Yessir. Coming, sir," bawled Nabbs, and he pushed Belle out of the room, but not before she had called out, "Daisy! See what you can do!" and Daisy had answered, "All right Belle, but I won't be responsible!"

Nabbs hurried Belle along a wide corridor and up what had been a fine old staircase. What color the stair carpet had been, it was impossible to tell. Like everything else, it was soft dust-gray. He knocked at an impressive but badly scratched door and thrust Belle inside with a muttered, "Miss Barclay, sir."

The Colonel sat in a winged armchair with one heavily swathed foot resting on a low stool. He looked tired, drawn, and old. It was evidently his study, for the walls were lined with books and he was sitting beside a large workmanlike desk which was littered with papers. He must, Belle reflected, have a lot of business to attend to what with his trusteeship of Orsett Park and probably other properties, his own land, the impending by-election and heaven knew what other duties, without having to concern himself in Hugo's love life. A big golden retriever came out from under the desk and padded over to Belle. It sniffed 'round her and then went back to the Colonel and sank down beside him with a tremendous worried sigh.

"Sit down, Miss Barclay. Forgive me for not rising. I have a touch of gout."

"From standing about in damp shrubberies, perhaps?" suggested Belle sweetly.

"Nothing of the sort. I have long had a theory, which I now believe to be proved, that these attacks are brought on by nervous irritation. Well, I have certainly had enough of that over the last few days. But to business. I underestimated you, Miss Barclay, or I underestimated the susceptibility of youth. Perhaps both. My nephew has genuinely fallen in love with you. I accept the fact and I am now ready to, as they say, buy you off."

"Has Hugo spoken to you?" asked Belle curiously.

"No. It is unnecessary. His behavior towards you yesterday was such that the fact cannot be doubted, and Professor Sweeting has spoken to me on the subject. Hugo has broken with his daughter. Whether it will last, how long it will last, I do not know. But I do know that I want you out of here at the earliest possible moment. I shall not haggle with you. I have already written out a cheque which is more than adequate for any sacrifice entailed on your part. It is yours when you leave."

"But, Colonel Gore," said Belle, "this is out of my hands. I did not want your nephew to fall in love with me. I cannot make him stop being in love with me. If I leave, he will follow."

"A woman of your undoubted resource can think up something," considered the Colonel. "I suggest a letter left for him telling him that I have paid you to go away, which is all you ever came for. That you were 'leading him by the nose' or whatever objectionable slang phrase you use, for just that purpose. It has the merit of being the simple truth. You can also throw in some facetious remark about his age and—er—lack of experience. At twenty-one I seem to remember that that would have finished me completely with any woman, and I fancy Hugo is not much different. What will happen then is anybody's guess, but that will not be your concern. With any luck, Hugo may be quite put off your sex for as long as a fortnight."

He broke off, and she saw him wince with pain.

"You don't look very comfortable," said Belle, "May I—"

"No you may not," said the Colonel rudely. "I'm not at all comfortable. I'm in damned agony. All I want is to get you back to London. Here!"

He handed her a check. Belle took it, but didn't look at it. Instead, she regarded him steadily. The straight black hair, black eyes, black moustache, darkly tanned face, crisp whiteness of collar and cuffs—obviously the trollops did not touch his linen—his well-shaped, well-kept hands— The lines running from nostrils to mouth and between his eyes would be very deep in a few years' time if somebody didn't smooth them away, she thought.

"Well?" snapped the Colonel, uncomfortable under her scrutiny. "What are you waiting for?"

"I still think you're taking a very big risk," said Belle, pleating the scrap of paper between her fingers. "I can take the money and still whistle up Hugo, you know."

The Colonel, in turn, studied her. "I was in the army for nearly thirty years, Miss Barclay. I've been in some tight spots in my time and one thing I have learned thoroughly and that is, who I can trust. For all your musical-comedy airs and graces, I trust you."

"The army may have taught you that, but it never taught you the power and determination of love, Colonel Gore," answered Belle and, still without looking at it, she shredded the check into pieces and dropped them on the floor. The retriever came and sniffed at them and looked ready to burst into tears. *Isabelle Barclay, Prize Fool of the Century,* thought Belle. *This is what I came for, just as he said. Those scraps of paper probably represented security for Daisy and me for years—perhaps forever if we started a little business and it was successful.*

There was a short silence.

"I saw you do that in *The Miss and the Miser,*" said the Colonel. "You've hardly even altered the dialogue. Good God! Do you never stop play-acting? Now I'm to be put to the trouble of writing another, I suppose?"

"Write as many as you like," said Belle, "I'll have none of them."

The Colonel's face darkened. "Very well. In that case you force me to take extreme measures. I warn you, Miss Barclay. *Extreme measures!*"

Belle's lovely, lustrous eyes regarded him steadily and he stared back at her. His hands tightened on the arms of his chair. Belle's breathing quickened and her color rose.

Anything could have happened.

What did happen was that there was a tremendous tattoo on the door and Nabbs erupted into the room.

11

Belle looked at the Colonel.

The Colonel looked at Nabbs in blank astonishment.

"Beg pardon, sir, but I can't be answerable, sir," gulped Nabbs. "The domestic staff has decamped, sir!"

"Ooh sir!" chimed in a breathless voice, and there was Daisy pushing in. "There was *black beadles* sir, swarming all over the food!"

"What? What?" snapped the Colonel.

"There was *black beadles* sir, swarming—"

"There was a *insect*, sir, I admit—"

"Nabbs!" said the Colonel, in a terrible voice, "do you mean that the canteen is *verminous*? That I will not tolerate!"

"Well may you say it, sir!" cried Daisy, all fear of the Colonel forgotten now that she could meet him, as it were, on her own ground. "There they was, them two, setting down there reading their fortunes in the teacups and you with a dinner party tonight! I gave them fortunes, sir. They've gone off with a flea in their ear and they would have gone off with two bottles of whiskey, five of claret, half a plum cake, a box of tallow candles, four linen sheets, eight dessertspoons and a mousetrap in their baskets, if I hadn't searched 'em first. That precious pair is robbing you of everything that ain't screwed down, sir, while he—" and she pointed a scornful finger at Nabbs "—he just sits there oiling your boots and letting them do it! You're lucky to have a roof over your head, sir! They'd have had that, given time!"

"They may have had a few things—" began the luckless Nabbs.

"Few things!" shrilled Daisy.

"Well, I can't be everywhere," exploded Nabbs.

Daisy swelled up, preparatory to, as she would put it, "not 'arf-giving him what for" and, out of the corner of her eye, Belle saw the Colonel wince again.

"Send a message down to Mrs. Culpepper, Daisy, asking her to get some of the village women to come and give a hand," she murmured. "Off you go now. You too, Nabbs."

She shooed them out, both too surprised to protest and, once outside, said, "Nabbs, has the Colonel anything to take for his—gout?"

"He's got a bottle the doctor left. An opiate or something. But he won't take it," said Nabbs, sullenly.

"Where is it?"

"On the table by the window. With the glass and spoon I left. I can't do no more. I can't *make* him take it."

"Well, I can. Carry on, Daisy, you're doing splendidly. I'll be down in a minute."

She returned to the Colonel and under his suspicious gaze measured out a dose from the bottle. "This right?" she asked, advancing towards him.

"I'm not having that muck," said the Colonel.

"Oh yes, you are," contradicted Belle. She sat on the arm of his chair, her arm slid round his neck and she turned his angry face towards her. "Take it without a fuss, and you shall have a Cupid's Comfort afterwards. Didn't your mama used to say that to you when you were little?"

"No," said the Colonel.

"Then it's high time somebody did," said Belle firmly, and held the glass to his lips.

The Colonel swallowed the draught without a murmur.

"There," said Belle and kissed him gently on the mouth.

The Colonel made no sign of having noticed it, but didn't seem displeased.

"I think you'd be better in bed resting until this evening," said Belle.

"Well, I'm not going to bed," snapped the Colonel, his old self again. "I'm busy, very busy and I haven't time for these domestic disturbances. If that woman of yours has got rid of my maids, you must take the consequences."

"I intend to," replied Belle. "This house wants a thorough spring-clean, and it's going to have it."

"You are not coming in here!" shouted the Colonel. "D'you understand?"

"We shan't have time," answered Belle sweetly, from the door.

She found her way down to the kitchen, which was filthy and deserted. On the table was a note.

Hes driving me back to get Mrs.C. and help and old clothes ect. Dont do nothing and *dont eat nothing*. Have sent man to do food away. Explane later.

Belle occupied herself by reconnoitring. The kitchen would have to be cleaned up before she could fancy any food prepared in it, and she wasn't all that fussy. *And* the entrance hall and passages. *And* the dining room, a beautiful old room but reeking of mustiness and damp, everything still shrouded in dust sheets. *And* a room for the ladies to titivate and leave their wraps. *And* the drawing room. Bathroom? She peered cautiously. Ugh! It was heartbreaking.

Then everything happened at once. Daisy, Nabbs, and what seemed like half the village under the direction of Mrs. Culpepper arrived. They were all agog with curiosity and chattering and squawking like a flock of starlings, but every one of them had obviously in her time been in service up at the House and every one of them was a spring-cleaner, *par excellence*, in her own right. Belle sighed with relief. At least that was the cleaning taken care of. Deployed by Mrs. Culpepper, the brigade set to work.

" 'Ere, Belle, I've brought an old dress for you," said Daisy. "You can't work in that one. There's a little room over here you can change in."

"Miss Sash!" shrieked a horrified Mrs. Culpepper. "Miss Barclay can't do nasty dirty work like this will be! 'Ow can you say such a thing?"

"We want every pair of hands we can get," said Daisy, but she sounded dubious.

"If the Colonel or Her Ladyship or His Lordship was to walk in here and find Miss Barclay on her hands and knees scrubbing the floor, I'd drop dead!" declared Mrs. Culpepper. "No, miss, don't you do nothing of the kind. Besides, you look a proper picture in that dress. It's a pleasure to see it in this old Dirty Dick's of a place!"

"It has gone to rack and ruin," said Belle. "And yet I was thinking how very pleasant it could be."

Mrs. Culpepper proceeded to mount a pair of steps and to tear down with gusto a number of greasy, garish Christmas Supplement prints, mainly of large dogs and tiny kittens, and middle-class angels hovering over orphaned crossing-sweepers.

"When I married Culpepper and came here first, the old Dowager Countess was living here. Grandmother to the Colonel she was, of course. She always had a soft spot for the Colonel rather than his brother, though *he* was a very pleasant gentlemanly lad, that I will say. The Colonel was always a bit sharp-like, even as a boy. She left the Colonel this house and the farms attached to it and all her money, and she was a wealthy old lady, they said. Bit of a miser, wouldn't spend a penny piece if she could help it, so of course the poor old place was run down right from the time I first knew it. When she died the Colonel was away in the army and he never worried about it. When he came home he stayed up at the Park. Wasn't until this year when he came home for good that he moved in here. But when a gentleman isn't married, as I've said to Culpepper time and again, things get neglected. Because they don't care, miss," breathed Mrs. Culpepper in Belle's ear, as if it were a state secret. "They don't see it like we do!"

Quantities of water were being boiled up in the great copper and clouds of steam suddenly cut off Mrs. Culpepper.

"Daisy!" cried Belle, as she dimly discerned that lady dashing by. "What about the caterer?"

"I was here when he came," said Daisy, "if you could call him a caterer. Bit of a boy, learning his trade, that's all he was. I sent him back with a message saying that Colonel Gore was having an important dinner party *with ladies attending*, and he wanted something more than a round of beef and a bit of turkey what was all that boy seemed to have in his mind."

"Supposing they don't come back?" panicked Belle.

"Course they'll come back," scoffed Daisy. "They're not going to lose an order like this. They dursn't."

Daisy was right. The caterers arrived in the early afternoon with the proprietor himself, sweating and servilely voluble, leading the procession.

"My profound apologies, madam! My orders were from the Colonel's man to supply food for a very *plain* dinner party for tonight. The man, in fact, insisted that the Colonel did not care for 'fanciful messes.'"

"I quite understand," soothed Belle. "The Colonel himself does not care for anything too elaborate but his guests, of course, do! Especially when there are ladies. So he has decided on a rather smarter affair. He leaves the menu entirely to you."

"And very glad I am to hear it," beamed the caterer. "I have brought our head chef, and he will do justice to the occasion, I assure you."

"I'm afraid the kitchen won't do justice to him," said Belle frankly. "All I can say is that, through the efforts of these good ladies, it is at least spotless."

To everyone's relief Alphonze allowed himself to be led in and, although he turned up his eyes in disgust at the primitive cooking apparatus, he evidently took it as a challenge. He clapped his hands and his retinue toiled in with hampers of poultry, herbs, eggs, fruit, saucepans, boilers, knives, canisters, sacks of sugar.

Belle quietly closed the kitchen door behind her and ran into Nabbs.

"Nabbs! I've just remembered! The Colonel's medicine! Do go up and see he has it, please."

"He won't take it," spat Nabbs.

"If he won't, say that I shall come up and give it to him myself," said Belle.

Nabbs stormed off.

Belle sniffed appreciatively. The smell of beeswax was

now taking over from the astringencies of carbolic and disinfectant.

"We've moved them old presses or whatever they were out of the hall like you said and into that back room," announced Daisy. "And we've got up that old carpet and made a bonfire of it. There's a lovely black and white tiled floor under that, Belle, and we've been through the Colonel's luggage—what he brought back and never unpacked—and we found some lovely bearskin rugs and we've put them down. Was that Nabbs riled! They look a fair treat. Mr. Culpepper come and swep' the chimley and we're getting a lovely fire going there. We've found plenty of logs and coal—well, there's plenty of everything, that precious pair had got enough in to help themselves to all winter."

"That begins to look real *wholesome*," came Mrs. Culpepper's comfortable tones.

"The curtains'll be dry enough to put up before the company comes," volunteered another voice, "though I fancy they may have shrunk something."

"I thought they was gray. I'd never have knowed they was that pretty rose color," said another. "You could have knocked me down when we'd got 'em out of the third water and it started to show through!"

"We're not putting the stair carpet back," said Mrs. Culpepper. "We're doing like you said and polishing the stairs. They aren't as I would wish to see 'em even now, but they don't look bad. It's lovely wood. Miss Bridgers sent her special polish down from the Park, and you can't get no better than that. Three months reg'lar applications of that and them stairs would be fit for the Queen."

Then there was the dining room to be inspected, where the great oval mahogany table and chairs were being polished with an energy which was going a long way to undoing the neglect of years.

"Fair drank that polish in, they did," announced the matron in charge.

"We've found the silver, under lock and key, praise be, or that pair would have had it. That Nabbs had to get the key from the Colonel. Mr. Culpepper's cleaning it up out the back. Can't beat a man for cleaning silver. Black, it was! And there's some wunnerful linen and china. She always had good china, the old dowager, I'll say that for her."

"Splendid!" applauded Belle. "Now, flowers. Lots of them. I'd better send up to the Park, I suppose."

"The Colonel has a gardener, madam," said Mrs. Culpepper, "and several hothouses. That Whicker, the head gardener, he grows some beautiful blooms."

"Why aren't there any indoors then?" demanded Belle.

"He won't pick 'em!" chorused the women. "Mortal jealous of they blooms. Won't have one picked."

They looked at her expectantly.

"Nabbs will have to go and see him then," decided Belle.

"He's gone off, madam! That Nabbs has gone!"

"*I* shall have to speak to him then," said Belle, and felt a tingle of pleasurable fear run through her audience.

Summoning up her courage she went out of the back of the house and made her way to where she could see the glint of glass in the late afternoon sun. The obvious course was to go back and get written orders from the Colonel, but her pride rebelled. He and Nabbs were hoping and praying that she would be beaten and would have to grovel for assistance, but she wouldn't. After all, Daisy had tackled the "precious pair" and the caterer single-handedly. She must not be found wanting.

Although the front of Orsett Court was devoid of any sort of flower, there were carefully tended beds of roses at the back and three large glasshouses inside which every color in the rainbow flaunted. Belle was not horticulturally minded, but she recognized orchids, lilies, tuberoses, freesias, malmaisons and beautiful trailing ferns.

Whicker proved to be an old man, stone-deaf either in reality or by intent. Belle strongly suspected the latter, and also that the Colonel's flowers found their way to Covent Garden and the proceeds into Whicker's pocket. She was suddenly coldly furious. How they all bragged about him, the Colonel who had won the V.C. and who was standing for Parliament. One and all they basked in his reflected glory and they let him sit up there in a dirty, moldering house, wincing with pain from gout or, as she strongly suspected, an old bullet wound, and robbing him right, left and center. She had been boiling up for this all day, and now she rounded on Whicker and in language which the Orsett Park ladies would scarcely have recognized as English, she ordered him to have a first supply of blooms up at the house in half an hour and to continue with the same number every fifteen minutes thereafter until ordered to stop—or else. And she explained "or else" in some detail.

An under-gardener wheeled up the first barrowload twenty minutes later. He had enlarged his vocabulary considerably and was open in his admiration of Belle.

When they had finished, it looked beautiful. Flowers, fires and candelabra defied the damp and gloom of years. The women collected their belongings and softly admired their handiwork. "Really looks as if someone cared about the old place at last," they said. The caterer reported that everything was going splendidly in the kitchen. He was supplying waiters and they were arriving at any minute. There was only the wine to choose, and that must be left to the Colonel. The Colonel had a very tolerable cellar.

"I'd better go and see him then," said Belle, feeling unutterably weary.

"No need, here he comes," said the man, and sure enough the Colonel was slowly but gamely making his way downstairs towards them.

"Good evening, Greaves. Yes, I will speak to you about the wine immediately. Good evening, Mrs. Culpepper, Mrs. Mix, Mrs. Gudgeon, Mrs. Toplady, Mrs. Venables—" He named them all, and they all gave little bobs and smirks. "It was extremely good of you to come at such short notice and to effect such a transformation. I am afraid I have been sadly remiss. Sadly remiss."

"It was all *her* doing sir," said Mrs. Culpepper, pointing at Belle and evidently determined to give credit where credit was due.

The Colonel turned and looked at Belle.

"Ye-es," he said, without much enthusiasm. "Well, you must now return to your homes, or your husbands will be thinking you have deserted them. Your services will, of course, be remunerated."

Heavens, thought Belle, stupefied, *I hadn't* thought *of paying them!*

"And Nabbs will get you all safely home. First of all, though, he must return Miss Barclay to the Park or she will be late. Thank you, all of you." And with a pleasant smile, which Belle had not thought him capable of, he walked off with Greaves.

Belle and Daisy were bowled back to the Park by a silently smoldering Nabbs. Both were too tired to care. Daisy laid out the pale lemon tussore silk, which left Belle's shoulders completely bare, pure white feathers adorned Belle's hair, her earrings looked almost like diamonds and so did her necklace. With her lips salved, her cheeks touched with rouge, her skin powdered, Belle looked radiant but, once more, felt unaccountably old.

Despite her efforts, she was late and only Hugo was waiting in the hall when she went down. Oblivious of the footmen he caught her in his arms and kissed her passionately.

"I haven't seen you all day," he murmured. "I *ran* back from that blasted shoot and all I could learn was that you were down at my uncle's and must on no account be disturbed. What's happened, darling? There have been the most extravagant rumors about you cleaning the Court from top to bottom single-handedly and swearing at old Whicker like a trooper. As if you would! As if you could! You're as soft and sweet as a kitten. You can barely scratch!"

He kissed her again and again. He looked incredibly handsome. Belle clung to him in the desperation of tiredness, wretchedness . . . she didn't know what it was. Hugo practically carried her out to the carriage and held her close all the way.

The sight of the Court blazing with lights, alive with "carriage" voices, smart uniforms, pretty dresses and bright faces, roused her. They were welcomed in the glowing, spacious hall by the Colonel, very upright and correct in full evening dress.

"I'm glad you managed to fight your way through the bats, Hugo," he drawled, with a sideways glance at Belle. "They are most troublesome at this time of the year and in this locality."

"Not to me, sir," said Hugo. "I think they're much-maligned little creatures."

Again Belle was struck by his easy, confident bearing. Had *she* done this? Well, she must have done. But Hugo was looking 'round, amazed. "I say, Uncle, what a difference. The old place looks really handsome."

"Miss Barclay was the *dea ex machina,*" said the Colonel. "I took little part in the proceedings, except to forbid them. I was laid up with an attack of gout."

"Have you taken your medicine?" asked Belle abruptly.

The Colonel looked at her. "Under your threat, *yes,*" he replied.

"What threat?" demanded Hugo.

The Colonel stared at Belle and Belle stared coolly back at the Colonel. Neither answered.

"Oh Colonel Gore, isn't it all beautiful?" lisped a childish voice, and a marshmallow Julia Sweeting slipped her arm through his.

"Very beautiful," replied the Colonel, looking at her.

"Julia! Julia! Oh, there you are! I only have to look for the Colonel and there is my naughty little girl!" came the ecstatic tones of Mrs. Sweeting. "Isn't she naughty, Lady Melton?"

"Yes," said the Marchioness shortly and sourly, and Belle had never felt so drawn towards that lady.

"You must not allow her to monopolize you, Colonel. Shoo her away the minute she bores you!"

"Colonel Gore is always vewwy nice to me," remarked Julia consideringly. "He isn't to evewwybody, but he is to me." And she rubbed her face against the sleeve of his coat.

Belle had a sudden vision of the Colonel's dark head forcing Julia's silvery one down into a satin pillow, of her small fingers locked behind his head, pulling it even closer, of his lips finding hers, of a long shuddering sigh. She felt violently sick, and how they all got into dinner, she never knew.

12

The birthday dawned. A perfect example of a hazy, lazy September day, ushered in, as usual, to the accompaniment of clicking curtain rings by Daisy and a volley of questions.

"I didn't wait up. You told me not to. But how did it go?"

"Very well indeed," said Belle. "The chef surpassed himself and everyone was delighted. I think the Colonel was in a lot of pain but he kept quite affable and made a very nice speech about Hugo and we all drank Hugo's health and happiness. Then Hugo made a very good speech back."

"What about that woman and that airy-fairy girl? What were they up to?"

"Never left him," reported Belle. "Actually, they made a handsome couple, he so dark and she so fair."

"Well, you're fair," muttered Daisy.

"Brassy fair. She's silver fair and out-of-this-world. She'd probably make him a very good wife. She'd do just as he told her, but she'd twine him 'round her little finger and get whatever she wanted."

"She'd what?" snorted Daisy.

"Twine him 'round her little finger. That sort always does."

"Not after the honeymoon," said Daisy, "and I doubt if then. You ought not to have said that to her, Belle. I wish you hadn't."

"Oh, in for a penny, in for a pound," said Belle. "He's going to take extreme measures against me anyway. He told me so yesterday morning. That's why he sent for me. He could see how the land lay, and he tried to buy me off after all. He gave me a check, and I tore it up. I must have been mad."

"First bit of sense you've shown," approved Daisy. "I always 'ated it, as well you know. That Mr. Arbuthnot ought to be put in prison for thinking up such a wicked thing."

"Oh well, there is one bright spot. Mr. Goldspink has struck a bargain with me. How would you like to go to New York?"

"I wouldn't."

"I shall go alone then. He's pulling strings for me over there. In return I give up Hugo and leave the field clear for Muriella. The joke is that I hadn't even got Hugo to give up at the time, but I have now so that's all right!"

She was amazed to see that Daisy wasn't enjoying the joke.

"And just how are you going to give him up?" she asked, pulling viciously at a tangle in Belle's hair.

"Easy. The Colonel gave me a few hints yesterday. Anyway, Hugo doesn't know me at all. He thinks I'm sweet and ethereal, an older Julia Sweeting. I could jolly soon disillusion young Hugo, don't you worry, old dear."

"You ain't going to marry him, then?" said Daisy, very intent on a recalcitrant curl.

"Of course I'm not!" cried Belle, exasperated. "I'm not a baby-snatcher! You sit down there in that servants' hall, Daisy Sash, swilling down tea and any damned tomfoolery they dish up to you. A new start in the States, that's what I'm going to have and if you've got any sense you'll come with me. Still, that's up to you. Now, am I ready? Have we got a prayerbook?"

"How you've got the nerve to enter God's House after the way you're going on," fumed Daisy, "I do not know."

Before the festivities commenced a short service was being held in the church built by Henry Lefroy, hence Belle's wish to be suitably equipped. The church was decorated with early chrysanthemums which glowed golden, and the sun poured through the stained glass.

Duty done, the fun started. Having worshipped the Almighty in a subdued hat, Belle now prepared to dazzle the peasantry in a straw cartwheel laden with flowers, ribbons and tulle bows. Her gown was of clinging rose voile with six flounces, and her parasol had a classy mother-of-pearl handle and silk fringing.

An enormous marquee had been erected, with flags fluttering from it. The village, their friends and relations turned out in force. The County arrived. A military band blared from the bandstand; the geraniums screamed scarlet, and, at midday, a salute was fired on the cannon in the park with the Colonel in command. The church bells rang, the cricket match and the fair got going.

Belle thoroughly enjoyed herself. Everyone knew that His Lordship was mighty taken with the actress and was agog to see her. Luckily Belle was used to being stared at, and her looks and easy manners, plus the loud commendations of yesterday's helpers, secured her enthusiastic acceptance. The men liked her bubbling laugh and her delightfully saucy trick of half-glancing at them. The country squires guessed dimly that they were meeting an accomplished flirt, and they went red and boisterous and liked it.

Just before luncheon the Duchess of Peckham arrived. Belle had been at a loss to picture the Colonel's ancient mama, but when she saw a bad-tempered-looking little old lady being wheeled across the grass in a sort of wickerwork bathchair by a footman, she realized that there was no other way she *could* look. The Countess hurried forward to kiss her mother-in-law and get snapped at in return. The Colonel came next and apparently got badly mauled. Belle drifted closer. The Marchioness, for once somewhat nervous, was stepping forward and attempting to kiss the old lady, but was held off with an ebony stick and commanded to say where "that Montague" was. The Marchioness hesitated.

"Drunk already, by God!" asserted the Duchess. "As drunk as a *owl*, I'll be bound! Where's Hugo?" She had a broad country accent and a very loud voice.

"Playing cricket," retorted the Colonel. "They have time for a few more overs before luncheon."

"Why ain't he here?" demanded the Duchess. "Only damn well come out once a year now, and he can't be here to meet me. Shockin' manners!"

"Can't. Fielding," barked the Colonel, and, seizing the bathchair, he wheeled it 'round towards a group of villagers who had crowded together for support. The Duchess knew most of them, and those she didn't know she demanded the full names and life histories of, supported by the testimonials of those who did.

"It's some time since we had the pleasure of seeing Your Grace here," said Mrs. Culpepper, who apparently constituted herself spokeswoman on all these occasions.

"Aye, and I doubt if you'll see me again, Minnie," sighed the Duchess.

"Oh ma'am, you'll be dancing at His Lordship's wedding, I know you will!" rallied Mrs. Culpepper.

"No, no, Minnie," contradicted the Duchess, although well pleased. "His Lordship will be dancing at my funeral more like!"

"Never you say it, ma'am," cried Mrs. Culpepper. "You're as bobbish as plenty half your age."

"Say, isn't she terrifying?" breathed a voice in Belle's ear. It was Muriella, eye-catching in a plain white suit with enormous black buttons down one side. "Even Mama is steering clear of her, although she would dearly love to be introduced to a duchess."

"Mrs. Sweeting is taking up her position," observed Belle. "Now this I must see. Let's get nearer."

The Progress was moving swiftly towards the luncheon marquee and Mrs. Sweeting and Julia were waiting at the entrance. Mrs. Sweeting was obviously determined to claim acquaintance with the Duchess, simply to spite Mrs. Goldspink. As the cavalcade approached, she sailed forth, all gush and goo.

"Your Grace! How well you are looking. You are an example to us all. I always say to the Professor, 'If only I can wear half as well as the dear Duchess of Peckham, I shall be perfectly content!' "

"Gore—it's that fortune-huntin' woman, ain't it?" demanded the Duchess, in a perfectly audible voice. There were supressed giggles all round.

"It's Mrs. Sweeting, Mama," replied the Colonel loudly.

"I knew it," said the old lady. "Well, she's had her corns cut by all accounts. I may not get out, but I hear what's going on!"

Mrs. Sweeting laughed nervously. "Your Grace is in such spirits today! Julia, dear! Come and pay your respects to Her Grace!"

A wide-eyed Julia tiptoed over and brushed a kiss on the Duchess' cheek.

"So you've let my grandson slip, have you?" gloated the Duchess.

A large tear rolled down Julia's face.

"It was a charming boy and girl romance, Duchess," cut in Mrs. Sweeting smoothly and in no way embarrassed by the fact that everyone was drinking in every word. "Both are now older and serious thought will have to be given to their futures. What will become of dear Hugo I do *not* know, but my Julia—I trust and pray— will soon be linked to a man of wealth and position, a man of authority and influence, whom she can respect, turn to for guidance and lean on in the dark pathways which lie before us all. A man, I venture to say, not unknown to Your Grace!"

Here, Colonel Gore stared at Mrs. Sweeting steadily.

"And not Hugo?" demanded the Duchess.

"No," said Mrs. Sweeting, gently.

"Well, thank God for that," was the rejoinder. "Where is the young rip, anyways?"

"Here I am, Grandmama," said Hugo, at that moment. "And how is my blooming beauty today?"

"Much you care," snapped his relative. "So you ain't a-going to marry that Sweeting gel then? Come to your senses, eh?"

"I have come for my luncheon, not to discuss my matrimonial prospects, you wicked old thing," said Hugo.

"But who are you going to marry then?" enquired the Duchess. "You've got to get an heir, you know, lad. That halfwit of your mother only had you. I told 'em it was putting all their eggs in one basket, but Orsett always was a fool with her. Should have had half a dozen. I did, and none of the coddling she got neither. If anything happens to you, it means Gore will get the title, and how's he going to get a wife and child at his age?"

The Colonel looked furious, and Belle felt compensated for the ill-natured remarks he had made about *her* age.

"Besides, he don't want to be an earl and go into the Lords."

"Well, I shall have to see what can be done then," said Hugo. He caught Belle's eye and winked.

"Who are you laughing with?" instantly demanded his grandmother.

"I wasn't laughing, Grandmama. I was smiling at Miss Barclay."

"The play-actress!" breathed the Duchess, swiveling round.

"Yes, this is Miss Barclay," said Hugo, leading Belle forward. "Miss Barclay, my grandmother, the Duchess of Peckham. My grandmother rarely leaves Bruton Square but she knows everything that's happening in the Shoveller, Orsett and Peckham families. Her spies are legion. It so happens that *our* Bridgers is *her* Bridgers' sister, but I don't suppose it signifies," he said suggestively.

"Decent-lookin' gel," was the Duchess' opinion after a prolonged and thoroughly ill-bred stare at Belle. "Pretty coloring. Is it natural, my dear?"

"Some of it," replied Belle.

"Some of it!" wheezed the old lady, suddenly and unexpectedly convulsed with mirth. *"Some of it!* Oh, I like her! Where do you come from, my gel?"

"London," answered Belle.

"London's a big place to come from," said the Duchess.

"Isn't it?" smiled Belle.

"Nice-lookin' gel, ain't she, Gore?" enquired the old lady conversationally.

The Colonel grunted noncommittally.

"Barclay sounds a Scottish name," probed the Duchess, returning to the attack.

"My father had a parish in East Lothian."

"Clergyman, eh?"

"Yes."

"Big parish?"

"Yes."

"Poor parish?"

"Yes."

"Don't sound as if there was any money in it."

"There wasn't."

"Fond of Hugo, are you?"

"Of course."

"Don't say much, does she, Gore?" asked the Duchess.

"Perhaps Miss Barclay does not wish to be interrogated in public, Mama."

"Come on then. I'm ready for my lunch if you ain't. No, Gore. You ain't wheeling me in. This 'ere gel can. We'll sit up at the top table, my dear."

So to Belle fell the doubtful honor of maneuvering the Duchess into place and settling her to the feast while she felt Mrs. Sweeting *willing* her to overturn the old lady and spill the consommé all over her. Belle, nothing if not dexterous and graceful, did neither. The Duchess became more and more attached to Belle and continued to question her.

"And how is that big place, London? I live there, y'know, but I never go out now. Nothing but foreigners and prostitutes, both sexes nowadays I hear. 'Ow's the new King settling down? And little Alex? Enamels her face. 'As a dreadful time with him. They say he tried to strangle her, and that's why she wears those dog collars of hers—to hide the scars. Lot of trouble she's had. That eldest son of theirs—well, it's lucky he's gone by all accounts. 'Ave you been to one of their levées yet? Can't be as bad as the old Queen's. They was hell. When was you presented, my dear?"

"Miss Barclay is an *actress*, Duchess," called out Mrs. Sweeting. "A play-actress. The old Queen, God rest her,

would never have countenanced an actress at Court.
Times have changed!"

The Misses Maltravers squeaked that indeed they had.

"What d'you expect 'em to do then?" shouted the
Duchess. "Daft fools, them Maltravers girls are," she
added in a loud whisper. "But an *actress*! You won't believe this, my dear, but I acted once with the old Ben
Rivers Traveling Company when they came to Wolver-
hampton when I was a gel. For a week. As a lark.
Several of us took part. If my father had knowed 'e'd 'a
killed me!" she recalled with relish. "Never enjoyed meself so much since. Acted! In britches!" she roared in
Belle's ear, flinging herself back in the bathchair, in a
paroxym of delight.

"She was the scandal of the county, my grandmama,
in her youth," said Hugo.

"And what if I was?" cried the old lady, becoming
more and more pleased. "Acted! In britches!"

"She's getting too excited," came a loud aside from
Mrs. Sweeting. "I think—"

"I don't care what you think," roared the Duchess.
"Take that pious, Bible-thumping face off if you want to
stay at my table or I'll— *Gore!*" she suddenly bellowed,
"What in the name of thunder are you a-doing with that
chit?"

"I was helping Miss Sweeting to a lemon sorbet," replied the Colonel stiffly.

" 'Ave you got your arm round her?" demanded his
mother.

"No, I have not," shouted the Colonel, apparently now
past all patience.

"Then what's the silly 'ussy leaning up against you like
that for? Sit up straight, miss. 'Ave you got a backbone of
your own or do you 'ave to use other people's?"

Julia burst into tears and Mrs. Sweeting started up.
Everybody went red with embarrassment except the

Countess, whose lips formed the words, "How diverting!" and Hugo, who was unashamedly enjoying it.

"'Someone to lean on,'" remembered the Duchess.
"That's it. That's the very words she used. That's the
'ussy who wants someone to lean on. I'll thank you,
madam, to get your daughter someone other than my
son to lean on—and in my very face too!"

"Julia! Julia!" shrieked Mrs. Sweeting. "She feels
faint! It's the heat! Oh, Your Grace! Oh, Colonel Gore!
Would you be so very kind as to help Julia outside?"

Rising like a well-trained carp to her cue, Julia fal-
tered, "I feel faint, Mama. Colonel Gore, would you be
so kind as to take me outside?"

A great deal of uproar followed, in the midst of which
the Colonel picked up Julia bodily and carried her out of
the marquee, with Mrs. Sweeting twittering around like
a distracted but delighted moorhen. Julia, Belle noted,
went limp in quite a professional manner and fluttered her
eyelashes beautifully. Belle got another helping of ptarmi-
gan and found the Duchess' eye upon her approvingly.

"That's right, my dear. I like to see a gel with a good
appetite. Not one of these mimsey, die-away crea-
turues like that Sweeting gel. What have you done with
her? Where is she?" she roared out as the Colonel returned.

"On a chaise longue in the shade with her mama and
Bridgers in attendance," replied the Colonel, taking his
place and resuming his luncheon.

"Heat!" spat the Duchess contemptuously. "No good
marrying a gel like that, Gore, no good at all for breeding
purposes. Been tight-laced from the cradle, I'll be bound.
I remember when I was carrying you—"

Everyone within earshot had by this time given up any
pretense at polite conversation and was staring open-
mouthed at the terrible old Duchess. Belle didn't see why
she should sidetrack the old lady on to more conventional

paths, but she was a kind-hearted girl and the shame of
the poor little Misses Maltravers alone was more than she
could bear. Skillfully, she began to entertain the Duchess
with an account of her trials and tribulations in the theater. Belle could always be an entertaining companion,
and in a few minutes the old lady was wheezing delightedly and even old diehards like the Marchioness were
graciously smiling. Anything, *anything,* rather than let
that dreadful old woman start off again, even if it meant
playing up to the despised actress! Very shortly afterwards, Mrs. Sweeting and Julia reappeared, anxious not
to miss anything, but this time Mrs. Sweeting prudently
kept Julia beside her.

The luncheon ended with a speech from a very merry,
red-faced farmer on behalf of the tenants. He remembered the day when his young Lordship had been born
and the day when his father before him had been born,
and how he had caught His Lordship, or His Lordship's
father, or even both (though at different times, Belle supposed) scrumping apples. It went on and on. Belle's
eyes started to close. However, even the longest speech
winds somewhere safe to its oldest cliché and eventually
they were out in the fresh air. The cricket match was
resumed—lethargically, but resumed—and the children
were shepherded away to be sick. Belle was commanded
to wheel the Duchess back to the house for a rest.

"Miss Barclay can't manage it," said the Colonel.

"Course she can!" snapped his mother. "Strong,
'ealthy gel."

Nevertheless the Colonel spoke to one of the footmen,
who followed at a respectful distance in case Belle got
into difficulties, and she was glad to have him there for
she could not have got the Duchess and the bathchair up
the various steps and terraces which they encountered.

"Well, my dear, what's been happening?" cajoled the
Duchess, like a friendly tiger. "Last week, Gore's not

marrying anybody and Hugo's marrying the milksop gel. This week, Gore's marrying the milksop and Hugo's marrying you. It won't do, you know."

"I'm afraid your grandson does fancy himself in love with me, Your Grace," said Belle, "but if you wait until *next* week, you will find it is somebody else again."

"That Yankee gel, let's hope," ruminated the Duchess. "That's who Gore wants and he's right. That place eats money. I should know. It ate all mine, and my papa left me a fortune. Connie's went, too. Gore has to dip into his own pocket now to keep it going. He can afford it, but Hugo can't always expect it of him. Besides, what with the expense of going into Parliament and doing up his own establishment, from what I've heard—and not beforetime neither—he'll have to call a halt."

"Does Hugo know?" asked Belle, a little startled.

"Lor', no!"

"I think he ought to know and I think he ought to be allowed some part of the estate to run. He thinks there is plenty of money available, and it certainly seems as if there is, but if he's treated as a child he'll act like one. He worships the place and I'm sure he'll be willing to make sacrifices for it, even the sacrifice of marrying sensibly, if it's necessary."

"Ummm," said the Duchess.

"However, it isn't my business," said Belle. "I can assure you, though, that I definitely shall not marry your grandson."

"You're a good gel, a sensible gel," approved the Duchess. "I saw that right away. But what about Gore and that Sweeting miss? That hurt me, my dear. Hurt me. He's the only son I've got left, you know, and I daresay you think I'm a sentimental old fool over the lad, but I've got a fondness for him. I don't want to see him tied to that whey-faced creature. What started it off? He's never took the slightest heed of her before."

"I did," said Belle modestly. "To get her mind off your grandson, I told her that the Colonel didn't want her to marry Hugo because he was in love with her himself, and she's been his shadow ever since!"

The Duchess laughed so much that the footman had to come and steady the bathchair.

"Serve him right!" crowed the Duchess in between paroxyms of alarming chuckles and hiccups. "Oh, you're a one, you are! I'll come to your hanging, I promise you, miss. I'll come to your hanging!"

13

Belle luxuriated in yet another warm scented
bath ("You'll wash yourself away!" warned Daisy), and
after some refreshing lemon tea and chocolate biscuits,
got to work. Her hair was brushed and curled into golden
ringlets all over her head, delicate maquilage was applied
to an already flawless complexion, and the dress which
had been made by Lucile, no less, was squeezed into.
It was of silvery lace and as tight in the waist as even
Belle could stand. It was extremely low cut and was cal-
culated to bring a valetudinarian's blood to boiling point.

"Do you think the Colonel will like it?" she asked Daisy
frivolously.

"I should think he'll drop dead," said Daisy.

He didn't, but he kept his distance. The other men
crowded around like wasps around a jampot. Hugo held
her as if he would never let her go.

"I say," said Captain Studholme, who came next, "things have turned out rum, haven't they? So it's you and Hugo after all? We're all jolly pleased about it, Miss Barclay. If only the Colonel would come 'round—and Tubby has high hopes of it, you know. He says he's so taken with the Sweeting that he'll soften up. Realize what true love is and all that bilge, so things look fairly hopeful."

The band was divine, the floor superb, the flowers and jewels dazzling, the gowns and uniforms gorgeous. The Princesses were there, disappointing in looks but lavishly surrounded by the usual royal aura of glamour and excitement.

The Duchess came in late on the Colonel's arm, when she was certain she would make the biggest stir. She was dressed in a hopelessly out-of-date bustle and sported a baroque diamond tiara, necklace and earrings, which could all have done with a good clean. Her hair was too dark and ringletted to be real and her rouge was lopsided but, nevertheless, she made a brave show. She greeted the flower of the kingdom in exactly the same way as she had the villagers and she then, to Belle's surprise, permitted Hugo to lead her on to the floor where, with everyone else at a respectful and admiring distance, she danced a stately Viennese Waltz. Belle was rather resentful when she recalled how she and the footman had had to haul the Duchess and the bathchair back to the house that very afternoon. The old witch could easily have walked! However—

"Where's that nice gel?" demanded the Duchess as the dance ended and everyone applauded. "I'll sit with her for a bit."

Nothing loath, Hugo led her over to Belle who, at the Duchess' peremptory summons to—"Come and regale me, gel," had to forgo her dance with the Lord Lieutenant of the county.

"Your Grace is looking like a king's ransom," teased Belle.

"These?" said the Duchess, patting the diamonds. "All in trust. Go to Peckham's son the second I die and, knowing him, I mean the second! Got nothing out of Peckham, dear. Nothing. Well, hardly nothing. But I've been thinking over what you said about Hugo. Sensible. Wouldn't go against Gore in the ordinary way. Respect his judgment as a rule, but sometimes he tries to override everyone. Going to help Hugo meself and I've told Gore so and that he must have a serious talk with the boy and make it clear how the land lies. I think the lad will turn up trumps. Now, where is he?"

"Here, Grandmama! Ready for another dance?"

"No, you saucy young monkey! Sit down here and listen to me! You're twenty-one now, Hugo, and for a birthday present I'm giving you that property of mine over at Malmesbury. It'll give you a nice little income of your own, so you won't have to run to your uncle for every penny. It was coming to you when I died, but it's no good hanging on to things when you're my age, and you've been kept too sheltered and on too short a rein, in my opinion. But no more of that. I've sent word to the lawyer fellow to draw up his infernal deeds and as soon as they're signed— it's yours!"

"But don't you see darling, it's a marvelous stroke of luck!" said Hugo against the strains of "In the Shadows." "I never thought the old girl would act in defiance of Uncle Piers. She's always fallen in with him before, whatever she says. We can get married and live quite comfortably. It will be only four years at the most. Personally, I think Uncle will give in anyway now. He'll see it's no use. It's all due to you, Belle. Grandmama actually *likes* you! And she never likes anyone, so that just shows how wonderful you are!"

He gazed at her with adoration.

"For the last time, Hugo, I am not going to marry you. If your grandmother thought there was the slightest danger of it, she would not have been so generous to you. And don't hold me so close, everybody's looking!"

"The last time!" echoed Hugo, ignoring the rest of Belle's speech. "Thank heaven for that! Now we can start making plans right away. Let me announce our engagement now, darling, please!"

"No!" cried Belle.

"I will!" said Hugo.

"Hugo, please don't! Please don't do anything tonight to spoil your party. Tomorrow. Well talk about it tomorrow."

"Promise?"

"Promise," lied Belle, who was old enough to know that promises, like piecrusts, were made to be broken.

The next dance on her little programme was booked to Mr. Goldspink. They played "Tell Me, Pretty Maiden" and Goldspink insisted on humming it as they danced, jarringly off-key. Not content with that, he kept looking at her slyly and chuckling to himself as if enjoying some private joke. Belle decided to tap him, as he evidently wished her to.

"This is the first time I have seen you all day, Mr. Goldspink. Where have you been?"

"I have been to London, Miss Barclay, on your behalf, seeing my old friend the theatrical impresario, Judge Kershaw, and *he* would like to see *you* at ten of the clock at Clarendon's Hotel next Monday morning when, I think— I *think!* Here! Lands' sakes! Miss Barclay! Don't faint! I beg of you, don't faint! Quickly! Into the conservatory!"

A conservatory opened off from the ballroom, and it was the work of a moment for Goldspink to support Belle in and close the door. He then settled her in a brilliantly cushioned basket chair under Goliath-sized ferns. The conservatory was cool, damp and deserted.

"I don't think anyone saw us," puffed Goldspink, looking very hot and bothered. "Anyone" being, Belle guessed, Mrs. Goldspink.

"I'm sorry, so sorry. I'm all right now. It was just the *relief*!"

"Now, now!" warned Mr. Goldspink. "Not so fast, young lady. I can guarantee nothing, but Kershaw is mighty interested. Mighty interested. Yes sir! If you suit each other it will mean leaving next week for the States. May I be so indelicate as to ask how you are situated financially?"

"Rock bottom," answered Belle cheerfully, "but I shall manage. I don't want to be under even more of an obligation to you."

"I admire your spirit, my dear, and I shall look forward to seeing you at the top of the bill when I return at the end of the month. I shouldn't say anything to your theatrical friends, though. Many of them would like your opportunity, but Kershaw has already let it be known that his list is full and he is making a great exception for you. He usually likes the youngsters, the promising newcomers, so that he can mold them but—well, I've talked to him. You don't mind leaving so soon?"

"No, the sooner the better. In fact, I'm leaving here tonight and shall lie low until we sail. Things have been getting—difficult."

"Lord Orsett?"

"Yes."

Goldspink looked worried.

"It's all right. If he follows me, he can only try the Diadem and my lodgings at Meadowgate Street and he won't find me at either. I'm so much obliged to you, Mr. Goldspink, and I hope that your daughter will enjoy being Countess of Orsett."

"Is that all the thanks I get?" asked Goldspink and, to Belle's amazement, pulled her into his arms and kissed her violently. Belle struggled free and managed to knock over some exotic shrub housed in an Italian jar. It made a terrible crash, they flew apart and Belle was back into the ballroom in a flash.

"Oh, there you are," said the Colonel, eyeing her suspiciously. "I believe I have this dance." He hadn't, but Belle was too flustered to answer and, anyway, didn't get the chance. For the second time in her life she was in the Colonel's arms, this time quite respectably on the ballroom floor. The Colonel had no love of dancing, but was passable. In any case, he had other things on his mind.

"My mother has broken the extraordinary news that she is making over her Malmesbury property to Hugo—apparently on your instructions—and has demanded that I allow him more say in the running of the Orsett estate—also at your suggestion. You're feathering your nest to some advantage, aren't you, Miss Barclay?"

"When you start treating your nephew as an adult," said Belle wearily, "you will find he behaves as one and that he will be as anxious to make as suitable an alliance as even you could wish."

"When he starts behaving like an adult, I shall be pleased to treat him as one," growled the Colonel.

"Then it's an impasse, and as the senior you must make the first move," decided Belle, and waved to Captain Studholme.

"You have been a thundering nuisance ever since you came here," muttered the Colonel. "And kindly keep your mind on your own partner. Your impertinence now beats all. I had occasion to warn you the other day that I would be forced to take desperate measures against you. I still intend to do so."

"You'll have to hurry then," laughed Belle. "I'm leaving for America next week. Judge Kershaw, the impre-

sario, has offered me an excellent contract in the States."
This was stretching it a bit, but it had the effect of causing
the Colonel to blink.

"America?"

"Yes, I shall be a real, live Belle of New York!"

"So Blackford Lefroy has simply been an amusing in-
terlude for you between engagements?" sneered the Colonel.

Belle went pink.

"Well," continued the Colonel. "America or the Ant-
arctic won't be far enough away for safety, Miss Barclay.
I have not finished with you by any means. I know who
wished Miss Sweeting on me, who has wheedled my
mother into what I consider a most imprudent action,
who has changed Miss Goldspink from a good, tractable
girl into what I can only describe as a hoyden, who invaded
my house, provoked my domestic staff and drove them
from the premises, and who caused my head gardener
to give notice. I am the subject of ceaseless gossip in the
village, while as for Hugo himself—his character has
changed from the amenable to the truculent. It is all
your doing. What have you to say for yourself?"

His dark face loomed frighteningly close and Belle
stared at him, wide-eyed. Then, in answer to her prayers,
the dance ended, and there was a diversion. The diversion, however, was not the result of any prayer of Belle's.

Hugo had entered the ballroom, accompanied by an old
Romany woman dressed in traditional fashion in a red
shawl, with hooped gold rings in her ears and even a foul
old pipe stuck between her teeth. She looked the most
malevolent old crone Belle had ever seen.

"Don't be alarmed, Miss Barclay," reassured Tubby
Arbuthnot, who was Belle's next partner. "It's only the
fortune teller from the fair. The village maidens have been
clamoring to consult her all day. She's quite harmless, I
assure you."

Like all stage folk, Belle was abominably superstitious and the sight of that dirty, gaudy figure struck terror into her. Belle *knew* that whatever the gypsy said would come true. She swayed on her feet and Tubby led her to a little gilt chair and hovered over her solicitiously.

"I shall be quite all right," Belle managed to say. "I shall just sit here quietly for a few minutes. I think I have got overheated."

To her relief, Tubby went off. Nearly fainting twice in the same evening! *I must be getting the vapors,* thought Belle.

"Would any young lady like to have her fortune told?" Hugo was asking, and laughing, actually laughing! "I've crossed the gypsy's palm with silver enough for the lot of you."

He was lost in the rush for a bevy of girls dashed forward, hands outstretched. Precedence had to be given to the Princesses, of course, who were promised fine, wealthy husbands, many sons and journeys over the water. The others had much the same, but didn't seem to mind. Some had initials given to them which caused consternation and giggles and cries of, "No, it isn't! It couldn't be!" And the gypsy went on glancing at soft white hands, her eyes every so often flicking up to look into the eyes of the girl before her.

Muriella, flushed and laughing, came and sat beside Belle. She was in pink again, but a hot, sizzling pink which dazzled.

"The old biddy told me that I came from across the sea. Fancy that, Miss Barclay! And I don't think she had heard me speak so my atrocious accent didn't betray me. Anyway, you'll be pleased to know that I'm not going back but I'm going to marry a titled gentleman and be deliriously happy! Julia Sweeting's to marry an old man and be very wealthy, and Mrs. Sweeting's practically turning cartwheels. She objected slightly to the 'old' and suggested 'elderly', but the old girl practically spat in her eye and insisted on 'old,' which was one for the Colonel because that's obviously whom she meant, or whom Mama meant her to have meant!"

"The Colonel?" echoed Belle. Keep the conversation going and pray that she wasn't remembered. The fascination of that alien presence in the ballroom made it impossible for her to leave and yet she couldn't face that—that *sybil!* She couldn't hear her future, couldn't bear to hear it. She saw Hugo looking round and shrank back behind Muriella.

"Why, surely you knew that Mama Sweeting has decided on the Colonel as a husband for Julia now that even she can see she has lost Hugo?" inquired Muriella. "Everyone's talking about it. I can't think how she got the idea, but she did, and now she won't let Julia get out of his sight."

"Does he mind?" asked Belle through stiff lips; Hugo was coming over.

"Doesn't seem to," said Muriella. "But I hope he fights free. I hate seeing the Sweeting so triumphant."

"Belle!" commanded Hugo. "Come and have your fortune told."

"Oh please, Hugo! I'd rather not."

"Oh you must!" squealed Muriella, and several others standing by laughingly insisted. Belle hated the lot of them.

"Go on," ordered Hugo. "I shall talk to Miss Goldspink." Giving her a little push, he sat down in her place beside Muriella.

Well, that was one good thing, and in a spirit of self-sacrifice, Belle went to hear her fate. The band had recommenced playing. It was an innocuous tune from *The Country Girl,* but Belle could never hear it afterwards without feeling sick.

The gypsy held out her own filthy hand and Belle

peeled off her glove and put her own into it. The old woman barely glanced at it.

"You are alone in the world. You are from the north of the kingdom. You have been forced to earn your bread in strange ways in great cities. You have known great poverty and the shadow of great poverty hangs over you still for all your fine feathers." There was unmistakable hatred in her voice as if she held some personal grudge against Belle. "But there is gold in your palm and it will come to you soon. You will marry a rich, fair young man who you have already met. You will face opposition from his family, but you will live to laugh at your grief."

She flung Belle's hand from her, raked her with a final vicious glance, and was gone. Belle shook from head to foot.

"It is all very diverting, is it not?" inquired a voice close behind her. It was the Countess, smiling and clutching several floating scarves about her.

"Lady Orsett," said Belle desperately, "I hope you won't think me rude but I want to leave by the early morning train. There's one about four A.M., the Colonel once informed me, and I have decided to take it."

"But of course, my dear. We have been delighted to have you, even if for such a short stay. I trust nothing has happened to discommode you?"

"Lady Orsett, you know why I came here, don't you? Hugo, that is, your son, told you?"

"Oh, yes," agreed the Countess. "It was most diverting but, of course, the best-laid plans as that horrid, immoral Scottish poet put it—silly Hugo has quite driven poor little Julia into the Colonel's arms by his apparent neglect of her and has, I fear, lost her for good. But it is very diverting that the Colonel, who was so against the match, should now be practically betrothed to the girl himself!"

"Well, you see how it is," continued Belle. "There is no further need for me to remain."

"No. In fact, it could become a little embarrassing as everyone now *does* expect Hugo to marry you," laughed the Countess. "I never guessed his play-acting was so good. You will not believe this, but Bridgers herself came to me yesterday with a perfectly solemn face and said that Lord Orsett was violently in love with you and that everyone knew it but me! She demanded that you be put into a larger room! I did not know how to keep from laughing. 'Well, Bridgers,' I said, 'we shall see!' "

"It must have been very amusing for you," said Belle.

"Oh, I am frequently diverted," smiled the Countess happily. "Everybody knows but me, indeed! Nobody knows *but* me would be more like it! However, if you really wish to leave, my dear, I will tell Bridgers and she will have your trunks brought up and packed and will arrange for you and your maid to be driven to the station. But I should like to see you again. Your handling of her Grace was masterly and a little bird has told me about Malmesbury. Do come again, Miss Barclay. Just telegraph me first and I will tell Bridgers. You know my dear, I sometimes wonder if Hugo will marry Miss Goldspink after all. He is getting quite attached to her. I *almost* think he is holding her hand. It would so please the Colonel."

When Daisy arrived in the Orange Room a few minutes later, it was to find Belle frenziedly throwing all her belongings on to the bed, tears streaming down her face, a half-written letter on the dressing table.

"Who's found out?" demanded Daisy.

"I've got to get away," gulped Belle. "Now. I can't stay here. Everything's got on top of me. Goldspink's arranged things with the Yankee, and I never want to see the old devil again, I *can't* go on deceiving the Countess, Hugo's going to announce our engagement if I don't get away at once— I'm trying to write to him now—that damned gypsy says I *shall* marry him, and the Colonel's dancing with Julia!"

"All right, all right," soothed Daisy. "You put your feet up for five minutes. I'll pack what's necessary. Mary can finish it and they can send it on after us, if you're in that much of a hurry. Oh well, its back to Meadowgate Street, I suppose?"

"Nothing so grand," said Belle. "We're lying low for a few days. I'm not having Hugo follow us. We're going to your sister Annie's in Hoxton!"

14

Once removed from Orsett Park, Belle's spirits revived. However, she steadfastly refused to discuss the visit or the note which she had eventually finished and left for Hugo, and concentrated her energies on settling in at Daisy's sister's.

Mrs. Kimmence's establishment was neither more nor less than a slum. Sumner Court was a dirty alleyway of terrace houses where neither sun nor fresh, clean wind ever penetrated. It stank of cabbage water. It swarmed with grubby children. Unemployable men squatted on its doorsteps, spelling out the racing results and occasionally kicking at the lean, greyhound type of dog with which the place abounded. All that could be said in favor of Sumner Court was that its inhabitants were a friendly lot. It was just as well, as the word privacy didn't exist. Daisy was terribly ashamed of it and of her sister, who had married an out-of-work taxidermist. A few examples of his art adorned the front parlor and proclaimed just why he was.

Mrs. Kimmence's front parlor was famous in Sumner Court, being sacred to The Piano. Had it not been for the respectability conferred by this instrument, which nobody could play, Daisy would have refused outright to go.

The rest of the house, except for the kitchen, scullery and the Kimmences' matrimonial chamber, was let to such impecunious souls who, Daisy said, had sunk below even the doss-houses and the Salvation Army Penny Sit-Up.

"You're getting a bit above yourself, Miss Sash!" remarked Belle. "Our taste of high life has gone to your head."

"Well, look at it!" despaired Daisy. "Why the 'ell you had to come here I don't know. There, you always did have these freaks."

In fact, the fortune teller had thoroughly scared Belle. She was obsessed with the idea that Hugo would find her, and she couldn't face the prospect. Despite the horrible note she had written him, which had drawn largely on the Colonel's suggestions, she was convinced he would realize it was a trick and would be searching for her at the Diadem and at Meadowgate Street. He would get no further, she hoped, and she was right.

On Sunday afternoon, Daisy made a brief foray back to Meadowgate Street to warn Mrs. Makepeace that their trunks would be arriving from Orsett Park and to arrange with her to store them until further notice, and was told that a gentleman had called shortly before, inquiring for Miss Barclay. Money had certainly changed hands and the landlady's partiality for more prompted some skillful questioning and throw-away remarks in their short conversation. The usually taciturn Mrs. Makepeace was exceedingly garrulous and could hardly bear

to part with Daisy. She even suggested a nice cup of tea!
*Yes, while you send that ginger-haired lad of yours to lay
information,* guessed Daisy. Daisy was up to such tricks.
She gave nothing away and, knowing her London, went
back to Sumner Court like an eel, twisting and doubling
up and down back alleys in case she was being followed.
She found Belle being entertained by Mrs. Kimmence.

"In six months he's stuffed one canary," shrilled Mrs.
Kimmence into Belle's sympathetic ear. "How can we
live on that?"

Nevertheless, from the bottles of stout consumed by
Mrs. Kimmence, Belle guessed that Mr. Kimmence's un-
official occupation of bookie's runner must be quite re-
munerative. And Mrs. Kimmence herself had a sharp eye
for business. Even though Daisy was her sister, she demanded a week's rent in advance before allowing them
into the little back room which looked out on to the
backs, cats and perennial gray washing of the inaptly
named Pleasaunce Road. Daisy's tarradiddle of their usual
lodgings undergoing alterations met with pursed lips
from Mrs. Kimmence.

"I thought she was doing so well," she objected. "Her
name was up ever so big outside the theater. Me and
Kimmence went to see it." The name, it transpired, not
the show.

"We shall only be here for the week, if that," said the
harassed Daisy. "And that's too long for me, Annie
Kimmence. We shall be sailing for New York any day
now."

For Daisy was going. "I'll have to," was all she said.
"I couldn't sleep at night wondering what was happening
to you out there." But Annie Kimmence found her crying
her heart out in the scullery and in a rare burst of sisterly
affection forced a glass of stout down her.

Even Belle noticed that Daisy wasn't her old self.

"What's the matter, Dais?"

"Matter? Matter? You putting our lives into the hands of that Yankee, that's what's the matter."

"What? Old Goldspink? He can't welsh on his part of the bargain. I'm still too much of a danger to play fast and loose with, especially now Hugo's got Malmesbury. Even now I could get Hugo back. Goldspink wouldn't dare risk it. You sure there's nothing else?"

But Daisy wouldn't look at her. "There's that fortune teller," she burst out. "She said you were going to marry His Lordship. She *said* so!"

For the fiftieth time Belle kicked herself for having divulged the gipsy's forecast to Daisy for, if Belle was superstitious, Daisy was a hundred times more so. Daisy was a glossary of omens and portents and had a fund of weird and wonderful tales of hauntings, dreams and prognostications which had come true in the most amazing ways.

"She said I was going to marry a rich, fair young man," corrected Belle. "She didn't say Hugo. We both jumped to conclusions. He's not the only one in the world."

"You've met him already," intoned Daisy gloomily.

"Well, there's—there's—Tubby Arbuthnot!"

"And his family would oppose you,"

"Old Mr. Arbuthnot certainly would, and that's putting it mildly. Do buck up, Daisy! Everything will be all right on Monday. I shall have to wear the royal blue, it's all I've got. Does it want pressing?"

She looked smart and winning on Monday morning and Sumner Court watched her go with pride. Only Daisy had another good howl in the scullery, and prayed desperately to her Cockney God that Judge Kershaw would turn Belle down, no matter what pressure was brought to bear by Goldspink, or even, if all else failed, drop dead.

However, the laws of the universe prevailed. Mr. Kershaw was delighted enough with Miss Barclay to imme-

diately sign her up and remained as hale and hearty as if
Daisy had never shed a tear. Belle found him a sweet old
gentleman and felt as if she had known him for years.
She came out of the Clarendon Hotel smiling and filled
with hope, and ran straight into Lawton who was strolling along with a rose in his buttonhole, lavender gloves in
his hand, and peace and goodwill in his heart.

"By all that's wonderful—Miss Barclay! I thought you
were still enjoying your great success at Blackford Lefroy!"

"And what little birds have been twittering to you, Mr.
Lawton?" responded Belle, as arch as he.

"Aha! Rather large ones, rather large ones!" said Lawton. Lawton must have heard the rumours of her engagement to Hugo or he would not be wasting all this affability,
Belle guessed. "You are looking in excellent health and
spirits, Miss Barclay, if I may say so," continued Lawton,
falling into step beside her.

"I am. I have just been offered a contract in America by
the impresario, Judge Kershaw, and Miss Sash and I will
be sailing for New York on Friday."

"Good heavens!" exclaimed Lawton, stopping short,
"then that is why—"

"Why what?" asked Belle.

"Nothing, nothing," replied Lawton, walking on again,
but with an abstracted air. He was obviously rearranging
his thoughts and studying his attitudes. He coughed delicately. "I had thought that—marriage was more in the
air than a resumption of your stage career."

He glanced at her sideways.

"Well, it isn't," said Belle shortly.

As the prospect of his being acquainted with a future
countess receded, so Lawton's gallantry began to
evaporate.

"My apologies, Miss Barclay. I wish you every success
in America."

He raised his hat and they would have parted there and then except that a terrible wave of homesickness for the Diadem, accompanied by fear of the future, swept over Belle. She held out her hand.

"Come, let's say good bye as friends, Mr. Lawton. I assure you that the thought of starting again in a strange country appalls me, but Mr. Kershaw promises me that the standards in the States are not so exacting as they are here and that I shall sail along on my London reputation alone."

"Kershaw said *that*?" cried Lawton. "From my acquaintance with him, I can hardly believe it!"

"Indeed he did. He is quite amenable to tailoring my roles slightly so that I have less singing to do. He's a sweet old gentleman."

Lawton looked affronted. "Neither would I have called Kershaw an *old* gentleman," he remarked stiffly. "I happen to know he is many years *my* junior."

"Then I should never have guessed it!" cried Belle, astonished. "It must be all those white whiskers!"

"White whiskers!"

"Yes, but I thought you said you were acquainted with him? Perhaps you are thinking of a different gentleman?"

"I assure you, Miss Barclay, that I know 'Judge' Kershaw, as he likes to call himself, perfectly well, and have done so for many years. He comes over here periodically and snaps up such promising young artistes, whom I and others have been nurturing, as he can find. He is a sharp businessman and I must confess I am surprised to learn that he has engaged you knowing that your contract with me had terminated. It is not in Kershaw's character to engage other men's—forgive me—cast-offs. I have been wondering if, perchance, Colonel Gore has had any hand in the matter."

"Colonel Gore!"

"Yes. He came to me last Saturday and asked if I knew Judge Kershaw and, if so, where he was staying."

"Colonel Gore?"

"Yes," said Lawton, eyeing her nervously, for Belle had stopped dead and people were looking at her curiously. "I happened to know that Kershaw was staying at Clarendon's and the Colonel visited him there. Miss Barclay, you look faint. May I call you a cab?"

"N-no, thank you," stuttered Belle, "I will return to Clarendon's. I—I want to see Mr. Kershaw about s-something."

"But he has gone. Returned to New York. He went on Saturday night. Did you not know?"

Belle stared at him blankly. "He can't have gone on Saturday. I've just seen him."

Lawton looked at her pityingly. "Miss Barclay, whoever you saw, it was not Judge Kershaw. The description you give is wildly inaccurate. Besides, he left on Saturday night. Colonel Gore told me so. He came to thank me for my assistance and in the course of conversation remarked that he had only seen Kershaw for a few minutes before he left for the States."

Belle tried to focus on Lawton but he dissolved into a swirl of red rose, lavender gloves and silver-topped cane. She couldn't say a word.

"A practical joke, no doubt," said Lawton from a long way off. "Very unpleasant. I will bid you good-day, Miss Barclay."

He swirled away into a larger swirl and Belle turned into a famous haberdashers and blindly turned over antimacassars until the world stopped crumbling beneath her feet. After a while she made her way back to Clarendon's where she was told, as she had expected, that Mr. Kershaw had checked out a few minutes before. He was not returning, as far as they knew. Had another Mr. Kershaw been staying at the hotel last week? inquired Belle. Oh yes, that would be Judge Kershaw, an old and valued patron. An American gentleman. No, they did not recollect having seen the second Mr. Kershaw before. No, they did not find the duplication of names a coincidence at all. Good morning, madam.

"Vic Slaney!" said Daisy immediately.

"Of course it was. Even I tumbled to it eventually. No wonder I felt as if I knew him. He was having the time of his life. He never liked me and to see me sitting there drinking in all those lies that anyone but an utter fool would have seen through—Oh Dais! I can't bear it!"

"I'll wring his bloody neck," vowed Daisy. "But why? *Why?*"

"He was paid to by—by *him!*" choked Belle.

"Who? Who paid him?"

"Colonel Gore."

"I don't believe it," breathed Daisy after a full minute's silent reflection. "No, not if 'e was to stand there 'isself and swear to it on a stack of Bibles, I wouldn't believe it!"

Belle blew her nose and sat up.

"Lawton told me that Colonel Gore went to see him on Saturday morning asking where he could contact Judge Kershaw. I had bragged to him on Friday night that I had been given a contract by Kershaw and was off to America this week. He said he was determined to get even with me because of all the trouble I had caused and this is how he's done it. He called on Kershaw and bribed or tricked him into leaving without seeing me. He then got in touch with Slaney—he would be easy enough to find, he was always in The Windmill or The Elephant—and paid him to book in at Clarendon's under the name of Kershaw to interview me when I turned up. After all, I didn't know Kershaw. The real Kershaw would have told him that soon enough. He even got the tickets for Slaney to give

me. If I hadn't met Lawton we should have found ourselves stuck in that benighted country without a penny
between us. It's not even as if he was going to leave us in
New York. We'd got railway tickets to go on immediately
to some town out in the West. I said I'd never heard of it,
but Slaney assured me that it was a new pioneer town
with a fine, new theater! And I swallowed that too! Now,
don't talk to me about your bloody wonderful Colonel
any more. I never knew anyone could be so—so
wicked!"

She put her head down on the cheap dressing table
again and cried bitterly. She felt wretchedly ill. Her eyes
were burning, her throat felt parched and dusty, her skin
tight. She ached all over.

"What we going to tell Annie?" was all Daisy could say.

"Nothing," gulped Belle, making a tremendous effort
and getting up. "We'll have a cup of tea and then we're
going straight back to Orsett Park. I'm having this out
with Colonel the Honourable Piers Henry Lefroy Lefroy
Gore, once and for all!"

15

There were no first-class tickets this time and no conveyance waiting at the darkening station, either, although Belle had telegraphed the Countess that they would be arriving on the six-twenty-five. Obviously the White Queen had already forgotten their existence and her own pressing invitation.

Ignoring Daisy's whimpers, Belle hired the station fly and ordered the man to drive to Orsett Park, but to stop at Orsett Court on the way.

"What are you doing?" hissed Daisy as they trundled off.

"You are going to the Park and are going to walk in as if you owned the place and will say that I am on my way. I am calling on the Colonel first and will follow you."

Daisy trembled all over.

"Let's go back, Belle," she begged. "You're ill. I can

see it. You're sickening for something. You're half-delirious. This isn't going to do no good."

Belle obstinately shook her head and fought to keep the waves of nausea down.

"You're—you're going to marry His Lordship, after all?" enquired Daisy timidly.

"No, I'm not," stormed Belle. "And if you say anything else about that blasted gypsy, I'll kill you. Now be quiet!"

Daisy sank back, white-faced, and they drew up at the front door of Orsett Court.

"Sorry, Dais," muttered Belle. "I feel foul. This all started so—so light-heartedly, despite my getting the sack from the Diadem, but now it's awful and frightening and unbelievable. But don't worry, old dear. You go on up to the Park. I know what I'm going to do here and everything will be all right, I promise."

She gave Daisy a hug and a kiss and watched the fly rattle off.

Orsett Court didn't look any livelier. It still skulked behind its shroud of ivy. However, a neat little girl answered Belle's knock and announced, with a giggle, that she was one of the Culpeppers and that she was helping out until the Colonel had got straightened out. "For we've heard, miss, that he's getting married! The Colonel!"

"And not before time," observed Belle, looking around.

"I'll tell him you're here," said the little Culpepper. "Mr. Nabbs has gone up to Lunnon on business for the Colonel. I don't know what it's all about but he's got a hangman's face on him. The Colonel went yesterday, and the day before. An' there's some gennelmen coming any minute to wait on the Colonel. Some deportation, Mr. Nabbs called it, about the Colonel going into Parliament. Pollin' Day's getting near now, miss. Coo! Ain't it *famous!*"

"You run along and tell him I'm here before the gentlemen come, then," ordered Belle, and the girl sped off. To Belle's surprise, she was asked to step up immediately.

The Colonel and his dog were in the Colonel's study. The gas was lit as it was now quite dark in the gloomy room. The dog came warily forward, tail wagging, licked Belle's hand and then, having done the honors, retired under his master's desk. The Colonel, as dark and expressionless as ever, confined himself to placing a chair for her and raising an eyebrow.

The chair, the Colonel and the gaslight all in turn wobbled about as Belle tried to focus her gaze on them, but she stuck to her part.

"Congratulations, Colonel Gore!" she said. "You've done very well. In a couple of days you've wrecked my chance of marriage and ruined my career. Through me you have also impoverished my maid, who is too crippled to find other work easily, but I suppose the good must suffer with the wicked."

"*I* wrecked your chance of marriage? My dear madam, *you* threw Hugo over yourself. I did nothing. Neither have I ruined your career. In fact, rather to my surprise, I have learned that it was already ruined before you came here. I am sorry to hear it. I wish you had confided in me. It explains much of your behavior."

"Lawton told you, didn't he?" demanded Belle thickly, wishing she had asked the little Culpepper for a glass of water before she came up.

"Yes, he did," admitted the Colonel.

"You saw him on Saturday?"

"Yes," replied the Colonel, looking at her keenly. "Are you feeling quite well?"

"Perfectly," retorted Belle. "How much did it cost you to bribe Victor Slaney?"

"I don't know Victor Slaney and I don't know what you are talking about," said the Colonel.

"I'm talking about your extreme measures, as you very

well know," said Belle. "I never dreamt just how extreme you could get. How *could* you have planned such an evil thing? Whatever you thought of me, what had you against my maid? What did you honestly think would have become of us—abandoned, penniless, in the wildest, most lawless part of a foreign country? A man could have worked his way back, probably enjoyed it, but *two women*? You hoped it would mean prostitution, didn't you? You wanted me dragged down to the depths because I had dared to flirt with your nephew and defy you. There's a lot more I could say, but I'll leave it at that. You are thoroughly despicable."

"If I am to take it that this incomprehensible tirade means that you have come back to attempt to extract from me the money which I offered you the other day, I can assure you that you are not getting a penny."

"I wouldn't take a penny," said Belle, and now she was dangerously quiet. "I want more than that. I want maintenance for life. I want a husband. And the only suitable one I know is—you!"

The Colonel's face changed sufficiently to indicate that he was astounded.

"Your best course is to marry me," continued Belle. "Indeed, your only course. Your moral obligations alone demand that you keep me for the rest of my life and if that doesn't weigh with you—as I don't for one moment suppose that it does—then you can look at it from your own selfish viewpoint, which would be far more attractive to you, I don't doubt."

Without taking his eyes from her face, the Colonel reached mechanically for a cigar. The dog sat on his feet and pressed hard against his legs. It looked distracted and shivered violently.

"If your part in this plot comes to light, and Victor Slaney is the least dependable of conspirators, however much you paid him, it won't look very pretty or do your election chances much good, will it?" Belle went on. "I should be sorry about that, but you know how quick political opponents are to pick on anything unsavory. I daresay I could soon find somebody who was—interested in my story. For another thing, if you don't marry and marry very soon, you are going to be *forced* into marriage with Julia Sweeting. If you don't think that Mrs. Sweeting isn't capable of it—she's already spread it around the countryside as far as I can make out—then you underestimate her. She's been balked once; she won't be again."

"My sole object in taking Miss Sweeting under my wing was to keep her out of Hugo's way when he did, at last, show signs of becoming bored with her," put in the Colonel.

Belle experienced an odd feeling of relief, but thrust it aside. "Maybe, but Julia is young and exceedingly pretty and most attractive to a man of your age. Still, for your own sake you must remember that she is a fool. You told me so yourself."

"A man can be perfectly happy married to a foolish woman," interjected the Colonel.

"Not with the added attraction of Mrs. Sweeting in close proximity as a mother-in-law," retorted Belle.

"I doubt if a woman can be perfectly happy married to a man she regards as thoroughly despicable," continued the Colonel, unheeding.

Belle ignored this thrust and continued with the piece she had learned by heart although it was difficult when your tongue felt like hot flannel.

"You have left the army and come home. You are going to be a member of Parliament, at least so everyone says. You are uncle to an earl, well-connected, rich. You will have to entertain. You will have to completely reorganize your domestic affairs. You can hardly have your important guests coming here to be served by Nabbs with —with *beer and pickles!* You have got to have a home, and to have a home with the full twenty-four-hour service which it demands, you must have a wife, and I consider I would make an excessively good wife for you. Think how I got the house round in just a few hours for your dinner party. And—and—people *like* me. I know you don't, but I can charm the old gentlemen, the ones you will have to keep in with to get on in your career. The fact that I've been on the stage might shock some of the starchy ones to begin with, but I can bring them 'round. You know I can. Popularity is my stock in trade. Even after the way you have treated me, I'm quite willing, in return for marriage, to serve you well and faithfully, to have your best interests at heart always, to run your house efficiently and economically, to make it welcoming and a place you can be proud of."

"Good God!" was the Colonel's eventual and pious response.

I won't go, thought Belle. *I've done it now. I shall just sit here. I* won't *go. I must think of Daisy. I don't care what he says, how hateful he is, he* must *marry me!*

"May I ask," enquired the Colonel at last, looking out of the window, "whether this remarkable offer includes what I believe are known as 'marital rights'? Or is it merely as a housekeeper that you offer yourself?"

"Definitely not merely as a housekeeper," retorted Belle haughtily.

"Then it does," said the Colonel, looking at her appraisingly.

Belle colored. "I hadn't noticed that you found me repulsive. That night in the shrubbery—"

"You made the first move," the Colonel pointed out. "Common civility alone forbade any—what shall I say—indifference?—on my part."

He went on smoking and the minutes ticked by. The dog sighed and regarded Belle pathetically. Just when Belle thought she must faint, there was a tap at the door, and Nabbs entered. He looked at Belle sharply, and then at the Colonel.

"Yes, Nabbs?" said the Colonel, stubbing out his cigar in a dirty brass bowl.

"There was no news, sir, but I've brought back a letter, sir."

He seemed ill at ease and handed the Colonel an envelope. The Colonel looked at it but didn't open it.

"And the gentlemen have arrived, sir."

"Good. Send them up at once. And you can drive Miss Barclay to the Park in a minute.

"I presume that's where you will be staying?" he inquired, as Nabbs clattered off.

Belle did not reply. She couldn't. There was a curious drumming in her ears now and the floor kept coming up at her. The Colonel got up and handed her her gloves. She managed to stumble to her feet.

"Upon reflection," said the Colonel. "I am inclined to accept your proposal. Your reasons seem cogent and businesslike. Sensible, in fact. In short, I agree. I will come up to the Park as soon as I can to make final arrangements and to announce our engagement to the family, but I cannot commit myself to a particular time. Ah! Come along up, gentlemen. My visitor is just leaving. You don't want me to come down with you, Miss Barclay, do you? Damned gout's playing me up again. Thank you for calling. Nabbs will drive you to the Park. Good evening to you. Now gentlemen, this way!"

Half a dozen portly gentlemen filed past Belle and the study door was shut.

So that was that. Belle was to marry the Colonel. Her future was assured. She felt nothing, neither relief nor triumph. Far from planning housewifely improvements to Orsett Court, she walked through it unseeingly. She longed for something to drink, her mouth was dry and her hands trembling, but she couldn't think straight and it didn't

cross her mind to find the little maid and order some refreshment which, as the Colonel's bride-elect, she was
fully entitled to do. She even forgot Nabbs and, letting
herself out of the house, started to walk towards the lights
of Orsett Park until she heard horse's hoofs and jingly
harness coming along behind her, and suddenly remembered.

"*He* said I was to drive you there. Get in!" ordered
Nabbs curtly, drawing up alongside.

Belle's temper boiled over.

"I'll thank you to keep a civil tongue in your head,
Nabbs. I'll have you know that I'm marrying the Colonel
and if this is a sample of your behavior you'll be turned
off. I don't care how long you've been his batman."

"You're marrying the Colonel," whispered Nabbs in-
credulously. *"You!"*

"Yes, me. And if you don't like it, you can find employment elsewhere. A replacement can easily be found
for you. Mr. Sledgeman, for example, seems an obliging
and civil young man. Miss Sash speaks highly of him,
anyway."

For a moment Belle thought she was going to get
Nabbs's whip across her face, but she stood her ground.
Then Nabbs broke into incoherent, bitter speech, the general burden of which was bloody women. They couldn't
rest until they'd dragged an honest man down. They used
the lures the devil had given them to twist a man's heart
out of his body and then they treated him like dirt. Led a
man on, they did. Just to see how many bloody scalps they
could collect and then cackle over it to one another. And
he never thought he'd live to see the Colonel come to such
a pass, neither. Him who could have had anyone, anyone
in the country, to say nothing of a very high-caste Indian
Princess who wore an emerald as big as a walnut in her
nose and had thrown herself at the Colonel's feet when
she heard he was leaving and begged him to take her too,

as his servant, as his woman, anything. Swore to change her religion and become Christian for his sake. What did the Colonel want with the likes of Belle Barclay? Her and her precious maid. They should set up in business together and fleece poor honest chaps, they should.

"That's enough, Nabbs!" ordered Belle.

"And you can walk up to the Park," ranted Nabbs. "And I hopes you break your bloody neck on the way!"

He dragged the horse round again, whipped it up and left her standing in a cloud of dust in the dark lane. *A good start,* thought Belle. *Faithful servant alienated for ever.* She walked on sustained by the thought that at least she could get a glass of water at Orsett Park.

16

Orsett Park was at dinner when Belle arrived. The butler met her and apologized for there having been no conveyance at the station but Miss Bridgers was off-duty for the day and without any doubt her ladyship had either neglected to read, or had instantly lost, Miss Barclay's telegram. In the meanwhile, Miss Barclay's old room had been prepared and Miss Barclay's maid was awaiting her there. The first footman, who had been hovering, escorted Belle up.

"Cor, there wasn't half a carry-on on Saturday when they found you'd gone," he confided, the moment they were out of the butler's sight and hearing. He was, Belle remembered, Sledgeman, the taker of bets, who seemed to have an eye for Daisy. "Old Vinegar Mouth said, 'Count the spoons!' and the others all clucked away. His Lordship went about looking like a month of wet Mondays until that Yankee woman started buttering him up. *She's* getting well in there, miss. Different girl she is these days. Don't fancy her meself, but she's got the money and she'd keep him on the straight and narrow. They sent for the Colonel of course, like they always do, but he'd gone up to town himself and didn't get back till late that night, and by *that* time Her Ladyship had 'remembered' that you had told her you was going. Her Ladyship enjoys her joke, you know."

"What did the Colonel say?" asked Belle, for the servants knew everything.

"Nothing, miss, that we heard," Sledgeman had to admit, "but he cut church yesterday and went up to London again. Don't know why, 'cos Nabbs is as close-mouthed as a oyster, but he didn't get back till late and a sweet temper he was in, so young Ethel Culpepper reported back. Then, blow me, this morning he sent Nabbs up! Tom Highbed said he'd caught the ten-fifty-five."

"He's just come back, with a letter for the Colonel," volunteered Belle absently. "It's election business, I suppose."

At the same time she was wondering about the gentleman who had called at Meadowgate Street. The Colonel had been in London on Saturday and Sunday, whereas she had taken it for granted that the caller had been Hugo.

"Did Lord Orsett go to London over the weekend?" she asked casually.

"No, miss. Moped 'round here like a dying duck on Saturday. Then the Yankee took him over and walked him 'round the shrubbery and held his hand under the table and all the rest of it. No, he hasn't been away."

Belle drummed her fingers on the bannisters, watched by Sledgeman with lively curiosity. So it hadn't been Hugo and it must have been the Colonel. But what had he wanted with her? And why hadn't he said? Sledgeman coughed and Belle came to with a start. Discussing her host's private affairs with his footman on a landing! Whatever next! Luckily Daisy popped her head out of the Orange Room in time to extricate her.

"If you haven't got anything to do," she snapped at the unfortunate Sledgeman, "you can go down to the kitchen and get Miss Barclay something on a tray. She's missed dinner."

Sledgeman gave her a spaniel-like look and melted away, leaving Daisy to pull Belle inside and remove her hat and coat.

"You'd better have a wash and get to bed," was her opinion, after a prolonged stare at her mistress.

"I'll have the wash but not the bed. Dinner will soon be over and I'm going down to the drawing room to show myself."

"You've got nothing to wear."

"I shall go down in this. It doesn't matter."

"I know you're out of your mind," muttered Daisy. "I know it."

Belle submitted to Daisy's ministrations thankfully and nibbled at the abundant meal brought up by Sledgeman.

"He's going to be disappointed!" remarked Daisy, surveying the hardly touched dishes. "He takes money with the visiting valets on how much you eat."

Belle ignored her. It was only when she was nearly ready to go down and was smoothing her eyebrows with a licked forefinger that she broke the news.

"By the way Daisy, I'm definitely not marrying Hugo, gypsy or no gypsy."

"I know *that*," was the contemptuous retort. "I was told *that* before I'd fairly got foot inside the servants' hall. He's going to marry that Yankee. They aren't half going on about it too. Lost a lot of money over you, most of 'em."

"Serve 'em right," said Belle callously.

"It's back to Annie's then, I suppose," said Daisy. "We should never have left. Waste of the train fares coming down, and you only took singles too. Returns would have been cheaper. What you going to do then?"

"I'm going to marry the Colonel," said Belle, minutely surveying her left eyebrow in the mirror.

Daisy's reaction couldn't have been more satisfactory. She fainted dead away.

Belle, jerked out of her assumed calm, flapped around helplessly, uttering little squeaks of alarm and fanning her fallen handmaiden with a towel.

"Oh my Gawd!" bawled Daisy, coming round and bursting into tears at the same moment. Belle stopped fanning with the towel and mopped up Daisy's enormous and apparently inexhaustible tears instead. "If only your sainted ma had lived to see this day," sobbed Daisy, falling unconsciously into the faithful servant's role in *The Girl & The Grand Duke*.

"I don't suppose she would have been all that impressed," said Belle. "She wasn't that sort of woman. And you never knew her, so stop making out that you did. She wasn't particularly sainted, either."

But Daisy wept on, clutching Belle and occasionally giving her a very damp kiss. "It's all right! It's all *right*! Such a gent. Looks right through you as if you was dirt. A V.C. A J.P. *And* an M.P., too, as good as."

"How you can praise him up after what he had in store for you I do not know," marveled Belle. "I'm only marrying him to get my own back on him."

"If he hates you as much as you say, then why should he ask you to marry him? Eh?" demanded Daisy, winking horribly.

"He didn't ask me. I asked him!"

"You WHAT?"

"I asked him. I said, it's the least you can do after ruining my life. After all, I said, your conduct won't look so good if this gets round, will it? The Liberals will make the most of it. And they will."

Daisy fainted dead away again.

There were no happy tears when she recovered this time. "He'll put us in prison. It's—it's *blackmail*! He'll summons you for this. He's a J.P. and a magistrate and he'll know how. *Oh Gawd!*" wept poor Daisy.

"He's getting a good bargain," snapped Belle. "Now, if you've quite finished fainting, I'm going down."

The ladies of Orsett were in the drawing room.

"My dear," fluttered the Countess. "Bridgers is away and I am totally lost. There is so much to do and I completely forgot to order the carriage for you."

"That's all right," said Belle. "Has the Duchess gone?"

"Yes, she returned to London on Saturday. She does not like being away from home for long, but I think all your other friends are here."

Friends! Belle nearly laughed aloud. The Marchioness was glaring through her lorgnette, the Misses Maltravers were looking askance, Mrs. Goldspink was heaving with some turbulent emotion, and Muriella was scarlet with—something or other. Unfortunate, as she wore a pillar-box red gown and an unnecessary number of rubies.

The other ladies, known and unknown, were in a little ferment of excitement and kept up a light chatter amongst themselves, but not too loud to drown out anything interesting that was being said. They hadn't long to wait.

"You have not been away long, Miss Barclay," observed the Marchioness. "Your return, I take it, was unexpected and precipitate?"

"Yes, it was rather," mumbled Belle. She suddenly felt dreadfully ill again and quite unable to cope with the Marchioness or, indeed, anyone. She wondered how she could get out unobtrusively.

"Nevertheless, much has happened during your short

absence," continued the Marchioness to a chorus of "So it has" from the Maltraverses.

"I think you will find Lord Orsett—*changed*," predicted the Marchioness, with a cruel smile. "Come to his senses, one could almost say."

Mrs. Goldspink stopped heaving and shot a grateful smirk at the Marchioness. Belle guessed that the Marchioness in her pleasure at her (Belle's) discomfiture, was having to profess an approval of the Goldspinks which she might not otherwise have yielded to. Still, rather a foreign heiress in the ranks of the aristocracy than a faded and impertinent musical comedy star.

"I am glad to hear you say that, Lady Melton," rasped Mrs. Goldspink. "I myself have thought that dear Hugo has changed for the better these last few days. He seems much happier."

"It is your daughter's doing then," said the Marchioness, graciously.

"It will soon be wedding bells," squeaked one, or both, of the Misses Maltravers, who instinctively knew the right time to make a prodigious announcement as against their habitual trite choruses.

"My dear Miss Maltravers!" cried Mrs. Goldspink, highly pleased.

"Oh *please!*" protested Muriella, more scarlet than before.

"They are quite right," boomed the Marchioness. "I do not as a rule approve of very youthful marriages, but Hugo is a young man for whom an early alliance—a *suitable* alliance—is essential."

"That is quite right, you know," said a voice softly in Belle's ear. She looked round and straight into the watchful eyes of Mrs. Sweeting. "Miss Goldspink *is* most suitable. Rather, perhaps, a *hard* girl, and certainly no beauty, but dear Lord Orsett's character, as I have always known, although affectionate, is *pliable* and he is too apt to become entrapped in the wiles of—er—unscrupulous persons. Miss Goldspink will soon put an end to that!"

"Good!" said Belle, looking at her hard.

"We have nothing but talk of weddings nowadays," continued Mrs. Sweeting, quite unabashed. "I vow I am quite bored with the whole thing. It is my Julia's sole topic of conversation! But who can blame her? To few girls comes such happiness as to Julia. Such an eligible, wealthy, distinguished *parti*—the Professor and I could not be more delighted! And so much to do! A fine old residence, but totally neglected as you discovered for yourself when you *cleaned through*! But, dear me, what am I saying? Nothing is official yet, but we must look ahead. A suitable staff must be engaged, builders, decorators—oh, the list is endless! Julia, my love! Have you yet decided definitely on the crushed gooseberry velvet in the large drawing room with the Watteau silk drapery?"

Belle thought that the Colonel should be grateful to her for saving him from the large drawing room, if for nothing else.

"No, Mama," piped Julia, "but I would like a lot of gold tassels!"

"Bless her!" beamed Mrs. Sweeting. "And she is quite cast down tonight because Constant Admirer was not able to come to dinner. Might it have been business connected with an important by-election, I wonder? But I must not give away secrets before the actual acceptance!"

'If 'Constant Admirer' is Colonel Gore," said Belle loudly, who now felt too ill to care about anything, "he is in no position to propose to or be accepted by Miss Sweeting. He is marrying me!"

She had never imagined such a sensation. Some part of her detached itself and sat there thinking how like Act III of *The Miss & The Miser* it was when Chloe Somebody-or-Other, a supposed skivvy but, naturally, a princess in disguise, had announced that she was to marry the richest man in London.

Mrs. Sweeting was beside herself with temper. Belle could not distinguish what she was saying, but Julia's voice shrilled out above the rest. "Mama! What does she mean? Does she mean I'm not to marry the Colonel either, Mama?"

"Be quiet, you—you *fool!*" screamed Mrs. Sweeting. And really, Belle could not blame her. To have an ageing actress capture not only the first of your child's prize conquests, but the second as well, must be more than flesh and blood could bear and be expected to stay ladylike on.

"Send at once for your man of business, Constance!" the Marchioness was ordering. "God knows what entanglement Gore is in—*if* this creature is speaking the truth —which I doubt. But send for him. In any event, take legal proceedings at once!"

"She is thoroughly unscrupulous," shrilled Mrs. Goldspink. "Anything in trousers! Why, time and again she *forced* herself on Mr. Goldspink last week. Forced herself! It has distressed him beyond anything. He has not known how to shake her off without being downright rude!"

"So that is why you wrote that *evil* letter to Hugo," came a venomous voice in Belle's other ear, and this time it was Muriella, now chalk-white amongst her crimson finery. "He showed it to me, but not to anybody else, poor boy! I wondered and wondered but I see it all now. It was the Colonel you were angling for all the time, and when you had got him you threw Hugo aside like an old boot! You found out that Hugo didn't have the money, didn't you? That it was the Colonel who had the fortune. And that's why you're marrying him!"

"Well, you're marrying Hugo for his title," Belle was stung to retort.

"I'm not! I love Hugo, I love him!"

And she did too, and Belle's letter, far from bringing Muriella the happiness Belle had hoped, had cut the girl to the quick when she had read it. She did love Hugo, and because of the suffering Belle had caused him, although it was for Muriella's own benefit, she would never forgive.

Meanwhile, all over the room, the fury continued unabated.

"This will ruin Gore!" came the Marchioness' boom. "Ruin him!"

The Countess, who had been looking about her apparently uncomprehendingly, suddenly knocked over a bronze nymph which held aloft an electrically lit torch. The nymph knocked out cold the elderly cousin who had been bawling "Eh?" at intervals for several minutes. The pug that she fell on (the unfortunate beast which had already had its paw scalded, thanks to Belle), bit a cow-eyed girl, whose mouth had gradually opened wider and wider until it could go no further, and the cow-eyed girl fell screaming into the grand piano in a crescendo of disharmony. The cow-eyed girl's mother swooned in the grate and set her false fringe on fire, and the uproar was complete. The Misses Maltravers clung together on their settee with their eyes tightly shut, squealing in unison. Everybody rang bells furiously and shouted commands and counter-commands and in the midst of the turmoil Belle walked out.

She ran full pelt into the gentlemen who were coming from the dining room and looking alarmed at the noise— as well they might.

"What on earth?" demanded Tubby Arbuthnot, who was one of the first on the scene.

"Peregrine! Peregrine! Do not be rash!" quavered his father. "Come back!"

But Peregrine had vanished into the fray.

"What is happening?" cried poor old Mr. Arbuthnot.

"Well may you ask, Mr. Arbuthnot," panted Mrs. Sweeting, who had followed Belle. "It is *her*! That—that scarlet woman!" She pointed dramatically at Belle who was trapped between the opposing forces. *"She is going to marry the Colonel!"*

"Caught him, has she? Damme!" remarked the Marquis.

"Melton!" came the Marchioness' awful tones, and her noble lord's look of faint animation vanished.

"Is none of us safe?" quaked Mr. Arbuthnot, recoiling from Belle with horror.

"The *tone* of Society must inevitably suffer," decided Professor Sweeting equably.

"Is that all you've got to say?" shrieked his wife. "When your daughter, your only child, has been jilted practically at the altar? *Is that all?*"

"Well, my dear—" began Professor Sweeting helplessly, but it was too late. Mrs. Sweeting laughed horribly and then cried and then screamed and then fell flat on the floor as rigid as a whalebone and drummed her heels on the Aubusson.

It was then that Belle saw Mr. Goldspink hovering on the edge of the crowd, and memory returned.

She pushed through the crush and went up to him, holding out her hand.

"Mr. Goldspink, I'm terribly sorry. All your good, kind offices have failed. I shan't be going to America after all, but I want to thank you just the same. The truth is that I kept my appointment this morning, at least I went to keep it—"

She broke off. Goldspink was staring at her as if he doubted her sanity.

"B-but you arranged it for me," stammered Belle. "You arranged that I should go to America."

"Cyrus, come away," ordered familiar tones, and Mrs.

Goldspink was there, looming larger than ever before Belle's terrified, yet hypnotized gaze. "This person is deranged. You would not believe it but she has been attempting to pass herself off as Colonel Gore's fiancée to us. Now it is your turn."

"A police constable should be summoned," decreed the Marchioness, her voice again rising above everybody else's.

"Poor creature!" muttered Mr. Goldspink, staring at Belle, and placing his arm protectively round his wife's waist.

"But you did," insisted Belle. "That's why you went to London on Friday and saw Judge Kershaw, and I promised you I wouldn't marry Lord Orsett!"

"Now it's Lord Orsett!" cried Mrs. Goldspink.

"Whoever next?" asked Mr. Goldspink, his eyes as cold and hard as pebbles as he stared at Belle. "My dear, you and Muriella must leave this unsavory scene."

"And leave you with this creature? Never! It is my duty to stay. I have watched her all the week trying to flirt with you, and now, right at the end, when her fantastic lies are crumbling around her, she tries to compromise you still!"

"I'm afraid so, my love," replied Mr. Goldspink sorrowfully. "I never heard such accusations."

Belle was now so ill that all thoughts, impressions and conclusions came through very slowly, but once they got through they were revealed in perfect clarity. In the midst of all the hullabaloo, servants running, dogs barking, people shouting—one fact stood out. *It was all Goldspink's doing!* He wanted Muriella married to Hugo, yes, but his chief objective was—Belle herself. He wanted her as his mistress. His overtures had proved hopeless, unnoticed, he could only resort to trickery. And what trickery! What she could now see was only the tip of the iceberg. What diablerie was being set up in the States to further emmesh her once she arrived, she could only imagine. Everything she had laid at the Colonel's door, Goldspink had done. Vic Slaney. Everything. The Colonel *had* known nothing. His visit to Kershaw had been made to the genuine Kershaw and must have been to try and trace her when she left so precipitately. He could have learned nothing there and must have thought that her talk of a contract was pure fiction. He must have gone to Meadowgate Street, but he had known nothing, and a great peace overwhelmed Belle. Even when an ungentle hand caught her by the shoulder and forced her around, she remained smiling serenely, overcome by thankfulness. The ungentle hand was Hugo's. He was white, strained and in a towering passion.

"You said in that damnable note that you had got what you came for. I couldn't think what you meant, but I see now that it was my uncle. You were determined to catch him from the start. I must have been asleep! You've been using me all the time and laughing yourself sick. Well, here's something else to laugh at!"

Before she could move or speak, he crushed her in his arms and kissed her so cruelly that Belle almost lost consciousness. She struggled for breath as he half released her, and the intolerable pain of his hold on her eased. She vaguely saw a blur of stupefied faces round her and then he flung her on to the floor and strode away. It was all so reminiscent of Act II of *The Girl from the Metropolis* that Belle fell automatically into the most graceful of attitudes and allowed herself to be supported to her feet, very beautifully, by Tubby Arbuthnot.

"Peregrine! Peregrine! I command you to come here this instant!" ordered his distracted parent.

"She's ill, sir," began Tubby in low, worried tones, but Belle shook him off and made a superb exit up the grand marble staircase, along the electrically lit landings with the thick, crimson carpets and enormous mirrors and portraits, to the safety of the Orange Room and Daisy.

"You knew best, Dais, after all. The Colonel had nothing to do with it. As innocent as a new-born lamb."

"I knew he was!" exclaimed Daisy, her face lighting up.

"It was Goldspink. I ask you! Goldspink! He was sweet on me, did you know that?"

"Everyone did," muttered Daisy, "including Ma Goldspink!"

"Well, I didn't realize he was that far gone. He tried a pass in the conservatory but I thought nothing of it. But he'd got it all worked out. His idea was to get me—and you, as you insisted on coming—stuck out in some frontier town in the States where his money talked big and I was down to my last dollar. He even checked on that, come to think of it. Then he would come along and 'rescue' me. You can imagine how."

"I warned you," said Daisy. "Time and again, I warned you, but you wouldn't listen, would you? I should think you'll go straight off and apologize to the Colonel on your bended knees for your wicked suspicions. Let's hope he forgives you so's you can start your married life with a clear conscience."

"*Start my married life!* You're mad! How do you think I can marry him now? He owes me nothing. We're off. We shall have to walk to the station, I suppose, and it's pitch dark, but we can get the last train. Come on!"

Daisy looked at her miserably. "If he said he'd marry you, then he'll stand by his word, Belle."

Belle rounded on her. "I daresay he would. He would say that common civility alone demanded it, I suppose." Her voice broke. "Do you think I'm going through the rest of my life living on the proceeds of a lie and the Colonel's gallantry? I genuinely believed he had got me into this mess and that the least he could do was to get me out. Now I find he was telling the truth and he's in no way to blame. I've got to get away. I can't face him ever again, Daisy. I can't! When I think of the things I said!" Belle shuddered. "Anyway, before I found out the truth, I told them all downstairs that I was going to marry him. Half of them were having hysterics when I came out. They still are for all I know. Do you think I'm going to marry a man whose relations and friends despise me and who'd cut us both? I just want to get out of here and die!"

"Me too," agreed Daisy dolefully, and a less distracted Belle would have noticed a very un-Daisylike little quaver in her voice, but Belle was too occupied—in trying to convince herself that a three-mile walk would do her the world of good—to notice.

17

It was very late when Belle and Daisy got back to Sumner Court, but Sumner Court kept curious hours and thought nothing of being knocked up at two in the morning by a neighbor asking for a cup of sugar or a twist of tea.

"Thought you was going to stay for a few days," remarked the canary-stuffer. "You could no sooner have got there than you turned straight 'round and come back again. Did they chuck you out?"

The Kimmences had never been told of Orsett Park and only knew that Belle was occasionally invited to join a nobby house party, and it was no good asking questions, Annie Kimmence, because you won't get no answers.

Belle lay on the bed, her head aching and her eyes burning. Daisy bustled around, talking volubly and coaxing the cheap little room into some semblance of home.

Only the sharp glances she directed at Belle now and again denoted her desperate anxiety. "We'll have shrimps for supper and blow the expense," she said, "and then, in the morning, we'll work something out. There's other jobs besides Lawton's."

"I wonder if he will marry Julia," murmured Belle.

No need to ask who *he* was. It wasn't Lawton.

"Course he won't," snorted Daisy. "You was in love with him all the time, wasn't you, Belle?" she asked timidly.

Belle stirred and muttered something.

Daisy breathed on the mirror above the chest of drawers and shone it up furiously with a sheet of newspaper. "I knew you was. Right from the start. And you never *really* believed that he'd had anything to do with that wicked Vic Slaney, did you?"

"I've been feeling so ill and queer all day, Dais. I don't know what's the matter with me, but everything gets so distorted."

"But you never believed that the Colonel—*the Colonel*—would sit down with that Slaney and hatch up a scheme like that just to get even with you?"

There was a long silence before Belle finally said, "No. Of course I didn't" and Daisy breathed a sigh of relief and went on polishing until the newspaper fell apart.

"It was just an excuse to go and see him again, I think. I wanted him to marry me. I didn't care how or why. Shameless hussy, wasn't I? Still, I can see sense now. It just wouldn't have done."

Daisy flicked at imaginary cobwebs and breathed heavily.

"It's all a damned horrible tangle," went on Belle, half-asleep. "And yet not much is changed. We're back where we would have been if I hadn't gone out to dinner with Hugo that night. *He'll* go on being a crusty old bachelor living in that mausoleum and fending off Mrs. Sweetings.

Hugo will marry Muriella, just as it was always intended that he should. Just as he would have done if I had never stepped in. It's Fate, you know, Dais, you can't alter things however much you try."

"Well then, we shall have the wealthy fair man along any minute," rallied Daisy, "so you'd better get up and get your face washed. You aren't half-crumpling that suit too. Come on, Belle, get up and let's get it off. Then I'll nip out and get the shrimps. Old Bellamy's open all night."

But Belle didn't want any shrimps. At this Daisy got frightened because she had never known anything to put Belle off her food, but she put on a bold front, said Belle was tired out and no wonder, she was ready to drop herself, and got her to bed with a stone hot water bottle wrapped up in flannel. She sat by the bed for what remained of the night watching Belle toss and turn, listening to her half-delirious moaning, dreading her high color, the beads of sweat on her forehead and the simultaneous shivering. As dawn came, Belle seemed a little easier and Daisy snatched an hour's sleep in the chair, but by mid-morning she was rambling again and her condition was such that Daisy was compelled to call in Annie, who was the acknowledged Sumner Court authority on child- and deathbeds.

Annie was of no comfort. Preferring drama above all else, her considered opinion that it was brain fever and that Belle's mind would go, just like Kimmence's aunt's did, was stated in tones of calm authority that would have befitted the King's surgeon. However, having chilled poor Daisy to the marrow, Mrs. Kimmence proved herself a competent and kind-hearted nurse. It was little enough that the poor woman had to enliven her drab existence (apart from the front parlor), and it was to her credit that she took to illness as others took to gin. It spoke volumes for Sumner Court that nobody, not even Daisy, dreamt of calling in a doctor. These short, sharp attacks were commonplace in Sumner Court and were consequent upon lack of drainage and appalling sanitary conditions. Belle, not being immunized against these particular germs, as were those born and bred in Sumner Court, made a sensational case. For three days she "hung between life and death" as Mrs. Kimmence put it but, "Dais and me took turn and turn about until the crisis came and then we watched together, for trust any sick soul to Daisy Sash alone that I would not, let Kimmence say what he will."

A Mrs. Tovee, Mrs. Kimmence's rival in these matters, managed to gain access to the sickroom for a few minutes before being ousted, but she saw enough to roundly declare that the poor dear had no more got brain fever than she herself had. A high temperature and feverish was Mrs. Tovee's opinion, but trust Annie Kimmence to exaggerate.

Nevertheless, one thing was sure. Belle Barclay was ill and, most of the time, delirious. Sumner Court, Annie, and Daisy vanished completely and in their place she was reliving her time at Orsett Park. Seeing the clear lake, the fresh green grass and trees, the glistening chandeliers, the immaculate linen and silver, the polished wood and gleaming glass. Everything that was cool and clean, still and silent. She kept trying to work out what they would be doing now, but time got so muddled and thought so confused that it worried her beyond anything and largely accounted for her delirium. The horses would be stamping in the stableyard and somebody else would be riding the sweet little chestnut. The gentlemen would be hidden behind the crackling pages of *The Times* and *The Morning Post*. The servants would be clearing the breakfast things. Mary, her streamers flying, would be flirting, bright-eyed, with the lanky footman. No, she wouldn't. It was nighttime. A candle was burning beside her. They would all be in bed. Muriella in that great white canopied affair, Julia in some pink muslin flounced cot probably, the Marchioness stiffly at attention in a whaleboned night-dress and the Colonel—the Colonel on an uncomfortable camp bed.

You're what all the chaps dream about in the desert. Half-remembered phrases came and went through her brain monotonously, but she could never quite remember who had said them, and this made her more restless than ever. *"Your reasons seem cogent and businesslike." "So diverting!" "As if I would let the brute get into its beautiful hair!" "You will marry a rich, fair, young man!" "Belle, I adore you!" "You're such a brick, Miss Barclay!"* 'Round and 'round and 'round they went.

It was early Friday morning when Belle returned to her senses. She felt unutterably weak but perfectly clear in her mind and she was amazed to see Daisy sitting beside her in a high-backed chair, fully dressed and sound asleep. A subdued snore on the other side drew her attention to Mrs. Kimmence.

I've been ill, thought Belle. *Good heavens! Poor old Daisy must have been frantic if she got Annie in. I wonder what's been wrong*. She cautiously moved her arms and legs and even that slight movement was enough to wake Daisy who flew up with a startled cry of *"Annie!"*

This woke Mrs. Kimmence, who critically laid her hand on Belle's forehead, peered into Belle's eyes, placed her ear on Belle's heart, and then solemnly pronounced, "She's come through!" At which Daisy burst into tears and fled from the room, leaving a delighted Mrs. Kimmence to assume an expression of lofty contempt for such an amateur, and in clear possession of the field. Thus it was from Annie that Belle learned the day and time, the debt which could never be repaid in golden guineas to Mrs. Kimmence, who placed her trust in the Lord and regular teaspoonfuls of weak gruel, and also that she hadn't half been talking funny but wild horses would never drag a word of it from Annie Kimmence. A shamefaced Daisy then returned and a regimen of convalescence was worked out.

"She'll not leave this room for another week, let alone sail for America," declared Mrs. Kimmence.

"We're not going," said Daisy. "Our plans have changed."

"Oh," said Mrs. Kimmence.

By the following Monday, Belle had so far progressed as to allow Daisy to absent herself for an hour or so to go to Meadowgate Street. Mrs. Makepeace had to be told that the rooms were no longer to be kept on and the luggage which they had left there was to be collected.

"You're sure you don't want to go back?" asked Daisy. "We could manage it for a while at least."

"No," said Belle. "Too pricey. And Daisy?"

"Yes?" said Daisy, pausing at the door.

"Promise me faithfully that you will not tell Mrs. Makepeace or anyone else where I am."

Daisy looked crestfallen. "But Belle—"

"You must promise me Daisy, on your honor, or I'll—I'll get up and move somewhere else before you get back!"

"But, Belle, we ought to let her know. There may be letters. Someone may have a part for you."

"Daisy Sash, don't be such a damned fool."

"Well then, what else could it be? Who would want to trace you? Are you thinking of the Orsett Park lot, perhaps?" demanded Daisy belligerently.

Belle colored. "I'm the last person they'd want to get in touch with. But I just don't want anyone to know. It's no use, Daisy. I've been ill, and I'm fanciful and you must humor me. You must promise me faithfully, however ridiculous it is, that you will not tell anyone where I am."

Daisy breathed fiercely but, in the end, with a very bad grace, she promised.

"And that you won't let anyone follow you here either," cried Belle, as Daisy was about to flounce out.

"Oh—all right! Blast you!" yelled Daisy and slammed the door so hard that the stuffed mongoose in the hall fell over.

Later that morning she returned and shut the aggrieved taxidermist's mouth by giving him tuppence to bring up-stairs the trunks containing the rest of their effects.

"Had anyone been asking for me?" demanded Belle.

"My stars! You're obsessed, Belle Barclay, that's what you are. Obsessed!"

"Had anyone been asking for me?" shouted Belle.

"No, they had NOT! Nobody had been asking for you. There were no letters. I've told no one where you are. No one followed me here. Is there anything else your suspicious mind can think up? I can tell you're getting better, you're that irritable. Shall we change our names? Would that make you easier in your mind?" she enquired with heavy sarcasm. "Though what Annie Kimmence would have to say—"

"That's not a bad idea," said Belle. "If only we'd thought of it before!"

If only! About an hour later, while Belle was hesitating between being Miss Mary Smith and Mrs. Diantha Framlingham-Rippon, Mrs. Kimmence put her head round the door and said, "There's a bloke down here to see you, Dais. Says his name's Mabbs or Nabbs or suffink. He's coming up!"

18

Belle was up and sitting by the window in the
remnants of her Orsett Park glory, a pretty pink peignoir,
lavishly frilled. Daisy had washed her hair the night before and it lay in soft waves about her head. The pink had
been lending a little color to her pale cheeks, but it was not
needed after Annie's announcement. She flushed crimson
and rounded on Daisy, who backed against the chest-of-
drawers and shook with fright.

"I didn't tell! I didn't tell!" she cried before Belle could
say a word.

"Then how has he found out?" hissed Belle.

The sound of Nabbs's heavy footfalls coming along the
landing seemed to reassure Daisy. "I promised not to tell
where you were, and I never," she retorted with dignity.
"I didn't promise not to say where *I* was, and Mr. Nabbs

has come to see *me,* not *you.* It may have escaped your notice."

"Then go and see him and get out of here," began Belle, but she was too late. Nabbs was in.

He reminded Belle irrestistibly of a lead soldier. Not that he was in uniform, but he always looked as if he were.

"Good-day to you, ma'am. I'm sorry to hear you've not been yourself, ma'am. With your permission, ma'am, may I have a few words with Miss Sash?"

"As many as you like," said Belle, beginning to wonder.

"Thank you, ma'am," said Nabbs politely. Then, swinging round to Daisy, he roared, "I'll stand no more of it, d'you hear? I've got a licence in my pocket and we're damn well going to use it. Now! Pack your traps while I speak to your mistress!"

"Well, you've got a hope, William Nabbs!" exclaimed Daisy, tossing her head, turning from paper white to rosy pink. "I'm not one of your native servants and I don't care if you've got fifty licenses with gilt edges in your pocket, I'm not marrying you!"

"Well, you're not marrying Sledgeman," vowed Nabbs. "I'll break your neck and his, first. You've turned me down twice, but I know why now, so get your things!"

"To hear you, anyone would think we was married already," retorted Daisy. "Well, we're not. I've been warned in time. Fine sort of husband you'd be, shouting and bullying. Get along with you!"

"Daisy Sash, are you out of your mind?" demanded Belle, whose eyes were as big as saucers and were now beginning to let in a lot of unexpected light. "Nabbs wants to marry you and you've refused him! What's the matter with you? Why not?"

"And leave you?" said Daisy. "A fine pickle you'd be in!"

"Not in such a pickle as I would be with you to worry about. To know you're settled will be the best tonic anyone could possibly give me." Seeing Daisy put on her stubborn face, Belle turned to Nabbs. "Take no notice of her, Nabbs. Drag her off and kick her into the nearest church. That's the only way to deal with Daisy."

"Him and who else?" jeered Daisy. "I'm not going to marry him, so you can save your tears. He'll soon pick up with somebody else. Probably got three or four heathen wives, so-called, if the truth was known."

Nabbs looked livid and Belle flung herself into the breach again. "I think you're being absolutely horrible, Daisy. For one thing, Nabbs has been hanging about all the week, I suppose, trying to find you, traipsing the streets, making enquiries. The Colonel must be furious. For all you know, he has lost his job careering off in search of you."

"No, ma'am," said Nabbs. "Colonel's orders."

"Colonel's orders?" echoed Belle faintly. "You mean, he sent you?"

"Yes, ma'am."

There was a long silence during which Nabbs gradually became more and more discomfited and finally said, "If you could give me a minute, ma'am—*alone*."

"Anything you have to say to her can be said in front of me," snapped Daisy.

Nabbs looked at her with a hangdog air but, seeing there was no relenting, he turned back to Belle. "I wish to apologize, ma'am," he ground out, "for the remarks which I passed the last time we met."

"What remarks?" demanded Daisy instantly.

"Nothing, Daisy," put in Belle quickly. "That's quite all right, Nabbs. I was to blame for inadvertently saying— well, I didn't realize how matters were between you and— well, I was as much to blame."

"What did you say to Mr. Nabbs?" demanded Daisy, now rounding on Belle.

"No, ma'am, I was to blame," persisted Nabbs. "There was no call for me to go on like I did, but you'd cut me on the raw like, even though you spoke in all innocence."

"I'll hear the truth of it," Daisy promised Nabbs ominously. "And I'll hear the truth of it from you too," she added, turning to Belle.

"You'll hear nothing, Daisy Sash, so keep your mouth shut," snapped Belle. "This is between Nabbs and me. Now, Nabbs, the Colonel—"

"After I left you, I went back to the Court," said Nabbs, giving her a look of heartfelt gratitude. "I hung around the stables for a long time thinking things out. I knew I couldn't stand it when you both moved in, having to see *her* every day ogling that Sledgeman or married to him, even if I was kept on: I'd made up my mind to give notice and re-enlist when the Colonel's visitors went and he came out and told me to saddle his mare."

"I *will* hear the truth, Belle Barclay," promised Daisy again, "and I have never ogled Mr. Sledgeman. Never!"

"You were always flirting with him," contradicted Belle. "You can't tell dross from gold, my girl." This was laying it on a bit but Nabbs thawed as he stood. He continued with his narrative.

" 'I'm going up to the Park, Nabbs,' he said. 'That letter you brought back from the Diadem is very interesting,' he said. 'Very interesting. There's something very smoky going on and I mean to get to the bottom of it.' Just then, up rides His Lordship. I got out of the way, of course, but I could see His Lordship telling the Colonel something and the Colonel looking like murder. After a bit he said something sharplike, and His Lordship went off as white as a sheet. Then the Colonel calls out to me, 'I shall be catching the early morning train to town, Nabbs. Pack me a few things. I'm going up to the Park now to see what's happening. I understand Miss Barclay left more than an hour ago without a word to anyone and must have walked to the station and caught the last train. I want to know why.' And from the way he said it I knew someone was in for a setdown. Well, I thought, I'd better take my medicine too, so I told him what had passed between you and me, ma'am."

"I'll hear the truth—" droned Daisy.

"I told him how the land lay and said that, with his permission, I intended to re-enlist."

"Ooo-er!" breathed Daisy, all eyes. "Was he *mad*?" As always, the Colonel's reaction to any situation was of breathtaking interest to her.

"He wasn't best pleased," admitted Nabbs. "But when he was mounted he said, 'I think you will find,' he said, 'that Miss Sash was unaware, when she rejected your proposals of marriage, that Miss Barclay is to become my wife. Her refusal was due to reluctance to leave Miss Barclay, as she thought, alone and, quite probably, in a foreign country. Having a great deal more sense than Miss Barclay,' he said, 'Miss Sash divined that the whole project was exceedingly suspect. If only she had come to me,' he said, 'with her suspicions.' "

Daisy's look of gratification transfigured her.

"Well," continued Nabbs, "that gave me the first bit of hope I'd had. 'Then sir,' I said, 'with your permission, I will accompany you to London, though how we're going to find 'em unless they've gone back to Meadowgate Street, I do not know.' 'Neither do I, but we must try,' he said, 'and when we do find them, you will of course apologize to Miss Barclay for the great distress you must have caused her.' And so I do, ma'am," ended Nabbs, "most sincerely. It was just that I thought you was putting her up to it, ma'am, you yourself seemingly playing off first one and then the other, that I didn't know what I was saying."

Belle produced one of her smiles, rather a tremulous

one but nevertheless a Barclay Peculiar, and this time Nabbs succumbed and promptly became her slave for life. Not that Belle noticed. She was hugging certain sentences of Nabbs to her heart. *"The Colonel's orders." "The Colonel looking like murder." "Miss Barclay is to become my wife."* At least, he hadn't repudiated her the moment she had left. *"He said something sharplike."* Hugo had undoubtedly ridden over after they found she had left, to acquaint the Colonel with the wicked claims Belle was making. But the Colonel hadn't denounced her as he could have done, as she had half-imagined he would. No, he hadn't. He had said he would marry her and he would have done so whatever Orsett Park thought or said. That blasted gallantry! But she couldn't hold him to it. She had seen and heard the effect of her announcement. She couldn't subject *him* to that. She could stand it but she wasn't going to drag him down to it.

"I don't know what happened up at the Park except that Mr. Goldspink was called back urgent to America," said Nabbs, giving Belle an old-fashioned look, "but I've been here all the week, and the Colonel's been up and down every day. We've had our heads against a brick wall. We could only try the Diadem in case you contacted them for anything and Meadowgate Street. Your traps were there and we knew you'd have to go back or send back there sooner or later for them. I've drunk so many cups of that woman's tea, I must have ruined my inside for life and then, when you come, I'm not there. Still, I was there ten minutes later and the old girl had got the message so—"

He broke off as Mrs. Kimmence appeared looking apprehensive. " 'Ere, Belle," she said, wiping her hands on the coarse sacking apron she wore, "there's ever such a toff downstairs asking to see you most particular and urgent. All done up like a fourpenny hambone and ever so nice-spoken."

Belle went ashen. "The Colonel?" she whispered.

"No, 'e didn't say 'e was a Colonel," said Mrs. Kimmence, "and don't look like one neither. Thought it might be one of your theatrical friends. Said his name's Lawton."

Nabbs's voice broke across Daisy's exclamation. "That's right, ma'am," he affirmed. "I've been 'round to the Diadem every day. This Lawton's been in quite a taking, seemingly, and we arranged that I should let him know if I had any news and he would do the same for me. I sent him word just before I came here. I'm sorry if I shouldn't have done, ma'am."

"That old devil," cried Daisy. "I'll go down and settle him!"

"If there's any settling to be done, I'll do it," contradicted Nabbs, plucking her back bodily from the door.

" 'Ere! 'Ere! Kimmence will have no rows nor trouble in this 'ouse," asserted Mrs. Kimmence, who was drinking in the scene with the greatest wonder and excitement, and whose words were so mendacious that it was fortunate that Belle and Daisy were too occupied with their own emotions to take any notice of her. Kimmence, as he was fond of boasting, would have fought anyone for tuppence, and he frequently did it gratuitously.

"Wait a minute," said Belle sharply. "It might be a part!"

"Belle Barclay, you mean you'd sink your pride and go back to that—that *pig!*"

"Yes, I would," said Belle. "Would you bring him up, please, Mrs. Kimmence? Daisy! You and Nabbs go out for a stroll. In the direction of a nice church, preferably."

"I'm stopping here," said Daisy, "and no one shan't budge me!"

"Very well. With your permission, ma'am, I'll station myself on the landing," said Nabbs. "If you want him thrown downstairs, I'll do it on the word!"

"This way, sir," came Mrs. Kimmence's voice. "Mind that broken stair, sir. Time and again the landlord has promised to have that seen to and time and again he has *not*. 'Ere we are sir. Miss B is up—ooh, but we've had our hands full with her, sir. Twice I thought she'd gone." The last remarks were in a somewhat lower tone than Mrs. Kimmence normally employed, which meant they could be heard all over the house but not actually out in the street. Then, flinging the door as wide open as it would go, she announced from the card which she was carrying by one corner, "Mr. Lawton, proprietor of the Diadem The-ayter!"

Lawton *was* done up like a fourpenny hambone, in a pale gray suit and with a pink rose in his buttonhole. He carried a gold-headed cane, exuded a faint scent of lavender—and was in a fine state of ingratiation.

"Miss Barclay. My dear. I regret to learn that you have been ill. When we met last week, I did not think you looked at all the thing, but you brushed my inquiry aside. I see now that I should have insisted on your taking a cab and returning to your lodgings. I bitterly regret my deficiency. However, if you could spare me a few minutes of your time—*alone*," he added, casting a significant look at Daisy, by the chest of drawers, who was doing her breathing act like a miniature malignant dragon, and Mrs. Kimmence, who was having some difficulty in closing the door.

Mrs. Kimmence scuttled off but—"I'm stopping," said Daisy.

Lawton looked appealingly at Belle, who merely smiled sweetly at him, so laying his hat and stick on the wash-hand stand, he drew a chair up close to Belle and bent forward earnestly.

Oh, crikey, thought Belle inelegantly. *He's going to apologize too!* And Lawton did.

"I need hardly say, Miss Barclay, how much I deplore

my part, unwitting though it was, in this sorry affair.
When a certain gentleman, who shall be nameless, came
to me and requested me to furnish him with the name of
a male character actor I believed, as I was indeed told,
that the person was required to assist in some charades at
Orsett Park. As it was intimated that someone who was—
shall we say, resting—"

"You mean, some down-and-out, ready to do *anything*
for money," burst in Daisy.

"I didn't—"

"And so you put that wicked Victor Slaney up to it.
He's as unscrupulous as anyone what walks this earth!"

Lawton patted his forehead with a large, silk handker-
chief.

"I put no one 'up to' anything, Miss Barclay, and Miss
—er—Sash. I had no suspicions. The gentleman, who
shall be nameless—"

"Goldspink!" spat Daisy.

"Was, as far as I was aware, of irreproachable conduct."

"Yes, yes," soothed Belle.

"My first sensation of alarm was when I met you last
week and learned from your own lips that you had been
auditioned by Judge Kershaw. Nothing of what you said,
Miss Barclay, rang true. Your description of Kershaw's
appearance and, indeed, character, were totally at vari-
ance with the reality. Your not knowing that he had left
the country. I confess, Miss Barclay, that while speaking
to you I convinced myself that you were making up the
whole episode for some reason of your own. Therein
lay my fault! I should have probed, made inquiries,
begged you to consider, advised your friends. The cir-
cumstance of *Colonel Gore's* interest in Judge Kershaw
should have alerted me, but, at the time, it did not."

"We could have been on the high seas by now," muttered Daisy. "Retching!" she added darkly.

"While returning to the Diadem after our meeting," continued Lawton, "I had time to consider and to feel uneasy. An uneasiness which was increased when Colonel Gore's man called on me a few hours later, with a letter, penned by the Colonel himself, begging for my assistance in tracing you. He said that he had no clue as to your whereabouts, apart from the fact that you had told him that you were returning to the States with Judge Kershaw, which had proved to be palpably untrue as he had discovered when he had called upon that gentleman, the previous Saturday. It was then that the whole infamous plot became apparent. I wrote to him at once, 'Had you only seen fit to confide in me earlier, Colonel Gore, but it is too late!' While his man waited I wrote down what I believed had occurred. In all good faith, *you* had seen a character whom you had believed to be Judge Kershaw, but who was, in reality, someone else entirely."

"Slaney!" mouthed Daisy. "A child would have tumbled to it before you did!"

"I blame myself!" lamented Lawton. "'I blame myself,' I said to Colonel Gore, and to Lord Orsett when he came to see me at the Diadem, and to the Marchioness of Melton when she was so gracious as to— Colonel Gore has waited upon me no less than four times during the last three days and his manservant any number of times. And always I was obliged to say, 'No news.' I have had searches made everywhere for Victor Slaney but the rascal has completely disappeared, and I am not surprised. I have heard that he is himself on the way to the United States, no doubt as payment for his services."

"Then I hope *he's* retching!" said Daisy.

"And then today, when I was giving up all hope, I received a message that you had been traced to this address and here I am, Miss Barclay, as I said, to make my sincere apologies for having so unconsciously played such an unworthy part in the affair. But all's well that ends well, as the proverb says, and another of my little birds has told me that you and Colonel Gore—"

He paused delicately, and it was then that Belle disgraced herself.

"I won't marry him, I won't, I won't!" she screamed, and burst into tears.

"Nabbs! Nabbs!" bawled Daisy.

Not only Nabbs crashed into the room, but Mr. and Mrs. Kimmence, Mr. Kimmence rolling up his sleeves, evidently preparatory to receiving tuppence and fighting anyone.

"He's upsetting her!" yelled Daisy. "I knew he would. Old Pickle-face!"

Through the open door, Belle could see half Sumner Court crowded on the stairs, and the sight brought her around quicker than anything.

"Now look," gulped Belle, taking a firm grip on herself, "everything is quite all right. Mr. Lawton is not upsetting me, I'm upsetting myself. Mr. and Mrs. Kimmence, Nabbs, and Daisy too if you can't keep quiet, please leave us alone. Mr. Lawton will be going in a minute and everything will be quite all right."

They all stood irresolute, but an uproar on the lower reaches of the staircase, gradually working its way up to the landing, caused a diversion.

"It's the perlice," cried Kimmence, hastily unrolling his shirt sleeves.

"No it ain't, it's a bum!" was the opinion of the group halfway up.

"A bum in that carriage!" came up a jeer from below.

"Just a minute, madam," arose the unctous tones of Mrs. Tovee. "I'll show you into the front parlor while you're waiting."

This was enough for the Kimmences, who broke through the crowds like a cutter through the waves. Even Daisy's family feelings were outraged by this unauthorized broaching of the Kimmence's state apartment and, with Nabbs in pursuit, she too rushed off.

Lawton got up and closed the door.

"I am most sorry, Miss Barclay, to have been the cause of yet further distress to you. I beg you will overlook it. I had understood—but I must tire you no longer. I would, however, be most obliged if you could assure Colonel Gore and Lord Orsett and, if possible, the Marchioness of Melton—to say nothing of the dear Countess of Orsett, of course, that I have been leaving no stone unturned to find you and that—"

"Yes, of course, Mr. Lawton," interrupted Belle. "Now I do feel very tired. I am sure you will excuse me."

Lawton rose and took her hand.

"I will say *au 'voir*, Miss Barclay. I am sure that in the days to come we shall see you on the other side of the footlights at the old Diadem gracing the audience as you graced my cast for so many years, and I shall always say, 'Ah, there has never been another like her.' Goodbye, Miss Barclay, and my best wishes for a speedy recovery."

Before he quite closed the door, however, he returned for a moment to say pleadingly, "You will, please, convey my sincerest regards to the *Colonel*?"

Belle nodded wordlessly and Lawton finally withdrew.

Belle had little enough time to ponder over this series of events before Daisy came in. She was carefully holding a glass in her hand.

"Get this down you," she ordered. "You must need it after seeing that old B."

Belle sipped the cordial gratefully.

"You don't think he's gone off his head or anything, do you, Dais? He was so—odd. Servile."

"He always knew the way the wind was blowing,"

muttered Daisy. "Drink all of that now! Here, I nearly forgot. He's brought these."

Running out, she returned almost immediately with a great bowl of hothouse blooms which filled the dingy room like a shout of sunshine.

"I've had to put them in Annie's wash-hand basin," she said. "Not likely that her or Kimmence ever uses it, so it don't matter. Don't look bad, do they?"

"They're gorgeous," whispered Belle, and felt her eyes fill with tears.

"Now then, stop that, you're still weak. You should never have seen him. I'll take 'em out if you don't stop that."

"Well, I ask you," sniffed Belle. "From *Lawton*. He must have gone off his head. And I'm to give his regards to the Colonel and tell Hugo and the Marchioness and the Countess how he's been trying to find me. When does he think I'm going to meet up with any of them? I'm hardly likely to bump into them in Sumner Court!"

"You'd be surprised who you can bump into in Sumner Court these days," answered Daisy drily, removing the glass from Belle's hand. "There's a pair of the Orsett Park lot now waiting in the front parlor to see you!"

As if on cue, the door was flung open and Mrs. Kimmence, who had renounced the sacking apron for a large, starched, white one, announced loudly, "Mrs. and Miss Goldspink." And then, not quite so loudly, but loud enough, "They're foreigners and I don't want 'em sitting in my parlor any longer. They been shaking the dust out of me dried grasses in the hearth. I caught 'em at it! And Kimmence swears they've got their eye on his stuffed weasel. Cheek!"

19

Mrs. *Goldspink and Muriella surged in, fol-*
lowed by Sledgeman, who was carrying two wicker hampers, and Nabbs, who, with his eyes narrowed, interposed
himself between Sledgeman and Daisy.

Both ladies had evidently dressed with care. Mrs.
Goldspink had not a single precious stone about her, and
Muriella was in oatmeal-colored tweeds. Nevertheless,
Mrs. Goldspink remained an imposing woman and the
oatmeal tweeds would have gone a long way to buying
up Sumner Court in its entirety.

"Put the baskets there, Sledgeman," commanded Mrs.
Goldspink. "We will unpack them ourselves. We came at
once, Miss Barclay," she added, "upon receiving the news.
That will do, Sledgeman."

"Thank you, madam," said Sledgeman. His face was
impassive, practically vacant, until he reached the door,

when he turned back and gave Belle a tremendous wink with his right eye and then, for good measure, with his left. Belle had only time for a fleeting smile before Nabbs took him by the collar and pushed him out. The Goldspinks were too busy delving into the hampers to notice the little pantomime.

"Champagne," said Mrs. Goldspink.

"Champagne," repeated Muriella.

"Champagne," echoed Daisy, laying several bottles reverently on the marble-topped washstand beside Lawton's flowers.

"Brawn."

"Brawn."

"Brawn."

"Beef tea. Careful now."

"Careful now."

"Careful."

"Fresh butter, three dozen new-laid eggs, a cheese, home-cured ham, grapes, nectarines—"

The room now took on the air of Christmas.

"We called in at Fortnum & Masons on the way," explained Mrs. Goldspink. "We, Muriella and I, are staying temporarily at the Orsetts' town house, so that we should be on hand. There," she concluded, surveying the provisions with a satisfied air, "that should take care of you until you are fit to travel back to the Park."

"I've no intention of returning to the Park," expostulated Belle.

"Oh, you must!" pleaded Muriella, for the first time since she came in looking directly at Belle. "You must! If it's anything that I said last week—and I know it must be—please forgive me. It was because Hugo was so very upset by your letter. I wanted to hurt you back! I was too stupid to realize, until the Colonel explained, why you had written like that."

"It was unnecessarily cruel," put in Belle. "Forget it. I'm sorry too."

"But the things I said to you!" nearly wept Muriella.

"That is enough, Muriella," ordered Mrs. Goldspink. "Miss Barclay was delirious and remembers nothing of the incident. Do not recall it to her mind. I myself made remarks which may well have been open to misinterpretation—as did others—but I have *forced* myself to forget them as I am sure Miss Barclay has too."

"Yes," said Belle.

"I knew it!" beamed Mrs. Goldspink. "You are a woman of the world and a dear, good girl into the bargain!" And she enfolded Belle in a very bosomy, suffocating embrace. "Now Muriella, we must go."

Muriella kissed Belle's cheek and smiled at her tremulously. "Thank you so much—*Belle!*"

"How is Hugo?" asked Belle, not knowing what to say.

"Oh—he's very well," was the stammered reply, and Muriella allowed herself to be swept off. Mrs. Goldspink's goodwill was still floating up as she went out of the street door.

"Open the champagne, Daisy, and let's celebrate," said Belle, after an awe-stricken silence. "I seem to be regaining friends all over the place."

"You can have a piece of brawn," decided Daisy. "It's full of goodness. Here you are. Eat it all and we'll see about champagne."

"Perhaps we'd better leave it for my next guests," giggled Belle.

"Thought you didn't want to see anyone?" snapped Daisy.

Belle pulled a face at her. "I've changed my mind. I didn't think they'd be fighting to come and apologize to me. Who's next? I'm getting impatient."

She didn't have to wait long. Mrs. Kimmence, resplendent in a neat black dress, frilly white apron and cap,

appeared in the doorway to announce in the most re-
fined tones, "Professor and Mrs. Sweeting. Miss Julia
Sweeting."

Professor Sweeting, small and jumpy, followed his
womenfolk into the room. He laid some heavy literary
magazines on the bed and squeaked, "Something to read,
Miss Barclay, to speed your convalescence."

"Nonsense, Theodore," chided Mrs. Sweeting. "Miss
Barclay would not wish to read those dreadfully dull periodicals. Julia and I have brought some fashion books,
which are much more interesting."

However, Belle smiled directly at the Professor, and he
sat thereafter in an almost visible glow.

"Mama!" piped Julia, who had been staring at Belle.
"Does not Miss Barclay look thin? She used to be quite
plump and pretty."

"*Julia*! Poor Miss Barclay has been very ill. I was distressed to hear of it from the dear Countess this morning,
Miss Barclay. Now come and sit quietly by her and tell
her how sorry you are."

"I'm vewwy sowwy, Miss Barclay," breathed Julia,
"that you have been ill. I have been ill, too, and Mama
also was ill."

"Nonsense, Julia. You have not been ill."

"I have, Mama," persisted Julia. "When the Colonel
came to the Park after you had gone, Miss Barclay, he
was howwid to me. He *shouted* at me, Miss Barclay. I
was petwified. And so was Mama," she added. "And
Papa. And we were ill."

"That is enough, Julia," said Mrs. Sweeting. "Miss
Barclay, the Professor has insisted that we come without
delay in order to correct the unfortunate impression you
may have received when we last met at Orsett Park."

"Yes indeed," said the Professor, sensing that something was required of him. "Indeed yes."

"I do not deny, Miss Barclay," went on Mrs. Sweeting, her color rather higher than usual, "that I spoke warmly. Very warmly. It was a Mother speaking, Miss Barclay. A Mother!" She wiped a small tear from the corner of a large blue eye and, as if in sympathy, Julia burst into noisy sobs.

Daisy rushed outside with a bottle of champagne and almost immediately Nabbs had drawn the cork with a satisfying pop and champagne was sparkling in the oddest collection of cups and glasses that could ever have been assembled.

"Isn't this nice, Papa?" asked Julia, accepting a chipped Coronation mug. "Although it is a funny place to live. I don't think I would like to live here, Papa!"

"JULIA!"

"Yes, Mama."

"Julia's experience of Life has been limited, Miss Barclay," apologized Mrs. Sweeting. "And that is partly why I spoke out as I did on that fatal day. Although, I freely admit, no offer had been made, the Colonel's attentions were such that the Professor and I, erroneously, as it happened, fancied they were more than neighborly. However, it has since been explained that his heightened interest in Julia was due to the fact that he foresaw her role in his own immediate circle becoming greatly enhanced in the near future through ties of matrimony—yes—but not through ties of matrimony with him."

"But it doesn't matter now, does it, Mama?" came Julia's shrill tones. "I don't want to mawwy the Colonel anyway. I don't want to mawwy anyone who shouts at me. And I'm not going to, am I, Mama? I have another beau, Miss Barclay," she confided, turning, all eyes, to Belle.

"Upon the Colonel freely and frankly admitting that his feelings for my Julia were warm, but not ardent," continued Mrs. Sweeting, "the Professor and I naturally withdrew at once from the entertainment of any such hopes as the union would have implied. The Colonel, in his turn, expressed himself surprised that Julia had not perceived the attentions, apparently blatantly obvious to everyone else," simpered Mrs. Sweeting, "of another suitor who had hesitated to speak, through some slight disparity of age, though not, believe me, Miss Barclay, of temper and understanding. But I must say no more now."

"I shall be ever so wich," lisped Julia. "Much wicher than Hugo, Miss Barclay. Much wicher than you, too. I haven't got an engagement wing yet, but I'm going to ask for a pigeon's egg wuby!"

"Julia!" expostulated Mrs. Sweeting indulgently. "But you see, Miss Barclay, it has all worked out for the best."

"That's what the fortune teller said," cried Julia. "She said I'd mawwy a wich old man—and I shall!"

"Not *old,* Julia," contradicted Mrs. Sweeting. "Elderly, my love. But I find, do not you, Miss Barclay, that these giddy young girls need an older, steadier partner?"

"Quite," said Belle, who was past having opinions on anything.

"Miss Goldspink hasn't got an engagement wing," interrupted Julia with satisfaction. "The Colonel won't consent!"

"Julia!" shrieked Mrs. Sweeting, and the Professor coughed alarmingly. "We must leave at once," cried Mrs. Sweeting, positively leaping up. "The Professor has a meeting to attend and I was quite forgetful of the time. Such a pleasant visit. Come, Julia! But it would be so suitable, Miss Barclay," she continued in a lower tone meant for Belle's ear only, "and I do hope that you will have no objection. Such an excellent *parti.* And such a high regard for you, Miss Barclay, you wouldn't believe! Yes, Theodore, we are coming! There is so much to do, Miss Barclay. Julia's bride's clothes and so on. We *did* wonder if you would be so very good as to be bridesmaid—or perhaps I should say matron-of-honor?"

Belle saw Daisy pour herself a generous cupful of champagne and toss it off as if it were water. She felt she could do the same. "That's very kind of you, Mrs. Sweeting, but I don't think—"

"Don't decide now," begged Mrs. Sweeting. "Pray don't decide now. Look through the magazines and see if any style particularly appeals to you. We should be most grateful for your help as you have such excellent taste. Julia and I always admire your *toilettes*. Perhaps we may have a little talk when you are quite recovered? I vow you look improved already! Does she not, Theodore? The champagne and, dare I say?, the company, have given you quite a sparkle. Julia! Ah, Nabbs! You are on guard, I see. Quite right. Take good care of her. Mind this stair, Julia. What a lot of people are outside! Good-bye, Miss Barclay!"

"Gawdstone the crows!" said Daisy, with feeling.

"Who on earth has she got hold of now to marry her Julia?" cried Belle. "And why should I object? And what would it matter if I did? Who can it be?"

"I should think she's learned to keep her mouth shut by now until she's got the banns called," said Daisy.

"And bringing the Professor along to make it all official!" continued Belle. "And the *Colonel* suggesting Mr. Whoever-he-is! I wondered how he'd get out of it."

"And the Colonel going for 'em! I'd have liked to have seen that!"

Belle sipped champagne in a contemplative mood.

"You heard what that girl said about the Colonel refusing his consent to His Lordship marrying Miss Muriella?" asked Daisy. "She talks such twaddle you don't take no notice, but they shut her up quick enough and Miss Muriella wasn't wearing a ring."

"I know. I noticed."

"Crikey, Belle, *he wants His Lordship to marry you after all!*"

"Oh Dais!" quavered Belle.

"The Marquis and Marchioness of Melton!" announced Mrs. Kimmence in tremendous tones, hurling the door back on its hinges. "This way, your Grace. Mind the torn linoleum, sir. We're 'aving the men in to relay it next week. Thank you, my lord."

The Marquis of Melton drooped vacantly by the washstand as he would have drooped anywhere—at a Court levée, the Day of Judgment, or Annie Kimmence's second-floor back. The Marchioness started to raise her lorgnette, thought better of it and came over to Belle. "My dear Miss Barclay. I hear that you have been ill? What regimen are you on? What have your doctors ordered for you? Melton wished to send for oysters, but I told him that they might be highly injurious. However, if they will not be highly injurious, then you shall have them. Who is your medical adviser?"

"Dr. Kimmence," replied Belle mischievously.

"I have never heard of him," pronounced the Marchioness. "Have you, Melton?" No, he hadn't. "I thought not. Sir Arthur Cleghorn must be summoned immediately."

However, upon Belle hastily saying that she didn't think it wise to change doctors in midstream and anyway she was practically recovered, the Marchioness allowed the subject to drop.

"Now, Miss Barclay," she said, settling herself in the old wicker chair. "I have a little bone to pick with you."

Belle's eyebrows expressed astonishment.

"You have been a naughty girl—a very naughty girl," said the Marchioness—*rather like a playful tigress*, thought Belle, mesmerised. "Of course, *I* could see that breeding was there. I remarked upon it to Melton. I know, Miss Barclay, that our young men must have their fling with the village girls. That is all very well in its way, but if the outcome is not legitimate—I trust I make myself

clear—then one cannot condone the marriage of that outcome with a member of one of our oldest families. I had
thought Miss Barclay that, as an actress, your birth had
been such an accident. High-spirited, aristocratic father
but, of course, unable to be publicly acknowledged.
Mother some tradesman's daughter. Instead I find that
your *mother* it is who had the lineage. Mary Margaret
Strathcaird, daughter of Strathcaird of Strathcaird. Poor
as church mice but allied, through marriage, with Melton
himself! Father, John Davenport Barclay, whose ancestry
I have been unable to trace, but who was, nevertheless, at
the time of the marriage, a clerk in holy orders, which is
perfectly satisfactory. There is nothing there," concluded
the Marchioness, "to shame any of us! And Mr. Arbuthnot agrees!"

Belle sat astounded. She had been astounded all day,
but this was astoundment past astoundment. She realized
that, in a roundabout way, the Marchioness was apolo-
gizing for her share in the Orsett Park fracas. But why?
Still wobbly from the fever and giggly from the champagne,
Belle went off into the realms of near-lightheadedness.
"Thank God!" she said solemnly. "Daisy! Champagne!"

Daisy looked at her, but got another bottle and took it
out to Nabbs. She returned to rinse out the crockery and
glassware so that all was ready when Nabbs came in with
the frothing bottle. The Marchioness was given the wine-
glass without the stem and the Marquis the thick glass
tumbler. Neither showed the slightest surprise or disdain.
Indeed—"Your health and happiness, my dear!" proposed the Marchioness. And—"Hear, hear!" said the Marquis, draining his tumbler. "Not bad. In fact, not bad
champagne at all," he pronounced. Daisy refilled his glass.

"You are no longer staying at Orsett Park?" enquired
Belle politely.

The Marquis suddenly exploded with laughter and his
champagne went down the wrong way.

"Melton!" roared the Marchioness, and he was instantly drooping again. "No, we returned last week," answered the Marchioness. "The country is delightful for a time, but one would not wish to remain there. We were at home in Berkeley Square this morning when the news of your illness reached us, and we came at once."

"And you will be staying there now?" asked Belle, making conversation.

The Marquis held out his tumbler surreptitiously, to Daisy, who refilled it.

"I—I trust so," answered the Marchioness. "It has been my home for many years, Miss Barclay. I cannot see that I could be happy living anywhere else. I am not a young woman to be uprooted, you know. However, what will be will be. Now, we must be leaving. It has been most pleasant to see you again and to have had our little chat. I feel that the air has been cleared. As you have no mother, dear, and Constance Gore, although a charming woman, is a fool, I do hope that you will consult me upon any little social matter on which I may be able to advise you in the future. Besides, with our mutual Strathcaird connections, I feel it only my duty."

Imprinting a kiss on Belle's forehead, one such as a benevolent basilisk might bestow, the Marchioness of Melton, followed by the Marquis, left Annie Kimmence's second floor back, caught her heel in the broken linoleum and hurtled down to the first floor back, taking part of the bannisters with her.

"I'll have another sliver of brawn," decided Belle tranquilly, as they listened to the uproar. "I've never had it with champagne before. It does seem a bit bizarre. I don't think it'll catch on."

"I won't go out," said Daisy, hacking at the brawn. "Nabbs will cope."

"Now look, Daisy. About Nabbs."

"You're *in*, Belle," interrupted Daisy. "If she accepts

you, you're in. She's *Society,* she is, though for all her
calling other people as poor as church mice, they say her
and him haven't got one penny piece to rub with another.
And she certainly don't spend it on dress, does she? But
she's got the *air,* if you know what I mean. You can see
that. She brought him a fortune when they was married,
so they say, but he ran through the lot. Drink and horses!
She was the niece of—"

"Don't get off the subject!" commanded Belle, cutting
into a rambling monologue of the Marchioness's fore-
bears. "*Nabbs!* I didn't know you were more than barely
acquainted with him. When did you have a chance to see
him?"

"You didn't care what was happening to me, what sort
of time I was having, did you?" said Daisy. "Not when
you were out all hours, enjoying yourself. I happened to
go out a few times with Nabbs. Why shouldn't I? It
seems to have given him ideas, though," she decided
gloomily.

"For goodness sake, let him keep those ideas. Why on
earth are you turning him down? Marry him, and look
sharp about it!"

"I didn't know your ma was the daughter of Strathcaird of Strathcaird."

"She wasn't. Unless he was a herring gutter in a small
way of business. But if that's how the Marchioness wants
it—you're getting off Nabbs again. He's really fallen for
you, Daisy. You can't treat him like this. As for me not
caring about what happened to you, what the devil do you
think I was doing this for? I wasn't worried so much
about myself, I can make out somehow, but about *you.*
What was going to become of you!"

"Damned cheek!" flared Daisy. "As if I couldn't earn a
crust without your help!'

But before Belle could do more than swallow the last
mouthful of brawn preparatory to having a fully-fledged

row with Daisy, the door was bumped open by the bottom of Mrs. Kimmence, who was anxiously peering down the stairs. " 'Ang on to Nabbs, mum. You'll be all right. Oh, what a worrit it all is to be sure. Me bannisters clawed down by a clumsy cow of a Marchioness, if ever I should say such a thing. You're quite safe, mum. 'Old on to Nabbs. There you are, you see. Safe and sound!" Then propelling the latest visitor forward with a hand in the small of her back, she announced, "The Countess of Orsett!"

"How diverting!" smiled the Countess from the threshhold.

20

"*Champagne!*" *approved the Countess, ad-*vancing into the room. She had a quantity of costly Russian sable trimming about her and took up rather a lot of room. "I should like just a little! Thank you. Delicious! Miss Barclay, you are a fraud. You are looking quite well, I declare. There was no need for me to have raced to your bedside."

"You have come from the Park, Lady Orsett?" enquired Belle, finding her voice.

"Yes. We had a wire from Nabbs early this morning giving your new address and adding that he understood you had been ill. The Sweetings set off immediately but I was a little late. The Misses Maltravers hindered me. They are most distressed to hear of your indisposition and have sent you this packet of Dr. Simpson's Ground Licorice Elixir with the instructions plainly inked on by Miss

Maltravers herself. They are convinced that you will find it of great efficacy. Their dear mother took it regularly before she died."

"How very kind," murmured Belle, resolving on no account to trust to Dr. Simpson if his Elixir had such dramatic results. "But, Lady Orsett, there was no need for you to have come at all."

"Oh, but I had to!" exclaimed the Countess. "I had to. Now why was it?" She sipped the champagne, thinking hard. Magically, her face cleared. "Of course! My dear, to my amazement, it was represented to me that I may have caused your abrupt departure from the Park last weekend! It was when you came in after dinner and said that you were going to marry my brother-in-law."

"Yes, I remember."

"My dear! *I was so diverted*! I have never been more diverted. Mrs. Sweeting's *face!* Mrs. Goldspink! The Marchioness! And the way you sat there so calmly! I thought I should have died. And when that stupid girl fell into the piano and her mother caught fire in the grate and Muriella flung the contents of the flower vase over her! And before I knew where I was, I was laughing so much that I was totally unable to stop. I have always been like that since a girl," she remarked modestly. "Anyway, as I say, it was represented to me that you might have taken offense at this and regarded it as a slight. For the life of me I couldn't see that this could possibly have been so, but I consulted Bridgers. Bridgers is outside in the carriage, by the way, and sends her best respects. And Bridgers said she thought you might very well have been offended. I have a great respect for Bridgers' judgment, Miss Barclay," confessed the Countess, "and if she is right, then I indeed apologize. But, really, I have never been more diverted!"

In spite of her determinedly sober face, she could not repress a little chuckle and the next moment Belle had joined in and then, despite making hideous faces in an attempt not to, Daisy herself. It was into the midst of this unruly gathering that the door flew open yet again and the stentorian tones of Mrs. Kimmence proclaimed, "His Lordship, the Earl of Orsett!"

"Hugo!" cried the Countess.

"Hullo, Mother," said Hugo. "Hullo, Belle. Daisy."

He was resplendent in military uniform and, at such close quarters, was overpowering.

"Champagne? I can do with a drop." He swished some around in the Marquis's discarded tumbler and emptied it into the improvised flower bowl. He then poured himself a generous helping. "Cheers!" They watched while he drained it. "Well, Mother," he said, putting the glass down and sitting on the bed, "so the old man sent you along to apologize too!"

The Countess bridled. "Bridgers thought it best," she said reproachfully.

"Daresay she did if she thought there was any danger of you getting your allowance cut. No flies on Bridgers. D'you mind if I smoke?"

"Certainly not, Hugo!" expostulated his mother. "Miss Barclay has been ill, and you can't smoke in her room."

"I don't mind," said Belle.

"Thanks, Belle," said Hugo gratefully. "You are a brick."

He lit a cigarette and drew on it in silence for a minute. Suddenly he laughed. "You are a brick. That was where we started, wasn't it? What an age ago, it seems. Now I'm to marry Muriella, if I'm allowed to—but I must first apologize for letting my feelings get the better of me when you said you were going to marry uncle. Still, *in vino veritas*. Perhaps the truth comes out in madness too." He threw the cigarette into the grate.

"Hugo, you are talking wildly," remarked the Countess.

"I know."

"What do you mean about marrying Muriella if you're allowed to?" asked Belle slowly.

"If I'm allowed to. In other words, if you give your consent," said Hugo.

"I don't understand."

"Don't you?" said Hugo, staring at her hard.

"Hugo," said Belle hesitantly. "The fortune teller!"

"Fortune teller?"

"Yes, at the ball. The one who said I would marry a rich, fair young man."

"Oh *her*. I'd forgotten her. I paid her to say that. I know what fools girls are for fortune-telling and I thought if she came out with that it might prejudice you a bit in my favor. I pointed you out to her before I sent you over. I wonder what the truth would have been? She was quite accurate with the others, so I heard. Do you want to consult her properly? I don't know where the fair has moved to now, but I could find out."

"Nothing would induce me," said Belle. "I just wondered, that was all." A wave of relief washed over her.

"She was no true Romany to let herself be bribed to tell lies," said Daisy severely.

"No, I suppose not," responded Hugo vaguely. "Although I seem to remember she was pretty mad about prostituting her art. It was fun in a way, wasn't it, Belle? But I'm of age now and Uncle's been talking to me, seriously, about the estate and the responsibilities it entails and so on, and I *do* have to marry money. One can't have everything one wants in this world. Muriella's a good sort, really, and I like her much more than I thought. Am I forgiven and can it all be forgotten?"

"Yes, of course," smiled Belle.

"Then I'll be romantic and have one last kiss," said Hugo, and dropping to his knees beside her, he put his arms round her and kissed her tenderly. "And if I know anything, that *is* the last I'll be allowed," he whispered, "but you know how I feel about you, Belle—always." Then, jumping to his feet, he said, "Well, come on, Mother. Here's your purse and your gloves. I'll see you to the station. Goodbye, Belle, and bless you. 'Bye, Daisy. Mother, your gloves! You've dropped them again. Hullo, Nabbs. On guard, I see. Quite right. Wait a minute, Mother. These stairs are a death trap. I'll help you down."

Belle and Daisy sipped champagne and remained each in her own private reverie until, like the Trump of Doom, Mrs. Kimmence proclaimed, as if life could hold no more, "Colonel the Honorable Piers Gore *V.C.*!"

"Never will Annie Kimmence forget this day!" said Daisy as the Colonel swung into the room.

He took one look at Belle, picked her up and put her into bed. He held her against him while Daisy plumped pillows up behind her, and even when that was finished he kept his arm round her and held her against his shoulder. Blissfully, Belle wriggled herself even closer. He smelt agreeably of cigars and leather.

"What the hell do you mean by letting that crowd of fools in?" demanded the Colonel. "Can't you see she's ill?"

"Well, sir," began Daisy nervously.

"Not you. Nabbs!" roared the Colonel. "What the hell do you—"

"Sorry, sir, but didn't know what to do for the best, sir," apologized Nabbs. "Miss Sash was here, sir, and if Madam had not been equal to it, sir, then she had only to call me and I would have had 'em out, sir."

"S'alright," murmured Belle.

"My God, she's drunk as well," said the Colonel with disgust.

"Only a little bubbly, sir," encouraged Daisy. "The best thing for convalescence there is."

"The sooner we get her out of this filthy back alley the better," said the Colonel.

"S'funny," said Belle. "You're the only one who's mentioned it. None of them said anything about my being here. Only Julia, and they soon stopped her."

"Well, as they did come, what did they have to say for themselves, eh?" demanded the Colonel, shaking her gently.

"Oh, they all had some wondrous tale to tell," yawned Belle. "Do you think they were genuine?"

"Don't suppose so," replied the Colonel. "But genuine or not, I don't care. The thing is—did they all apologize to you for their disgusting conduct last Saturday?"

"All except the Marchioness, and she nearly did."

"Then that's as much as we can expect from her," decided the Colonel.

"What did Hugo mean when he said that *with my consent* he would marry Muriella?"

"You forget," said the Colonel. "Hugo has to have my consent to marry."

"But you wanted him to marry Muriella! Why should you withhold permission now? And what have *I* got to do with it?"

Meeting his eyes, she went crimson and, in her confusion, went back into the shelter of his arm, hiding her face against his shoulder.

"I have the greatest reservations about allowing the Goldspink family to become allied to mine," said the Colonel. "I consider Goldspink's behavior extraordinary to say the least, and so I've told him. I have never heard anything so extraordinary. On the other hand, *my* doubts have served to kindle Hugo's enthusiasm, as perhaps I should have expected. He seems to be finding much to admire in Miss Goldspink suddenly." He gave one of his abrupt laughs. "Well, what do you think of it?"

"I think Muriella will make him an excellent wife, she's hopelessly in love with him," said Belle, "but how about the money? Will Mr. Goldspink—" She paused, uncertain of how to continue.

"Goldspink has gone back to the States on pressing business. I doubt if he will be seen very much in this country in the future. If he is, he will be treated, as far as we are concerned, with civil politeness. As for the money. It comes from *Mrs.* Goldspink. She was the sole heiress of a man who invented a type of fastening for—ahem—some item of ladies' underwear. I have no details but I believe that Mrs. Goldspink draws royalties for eternity. Mr. Goldspink is a shrewd enough businessman, but his start was owed entirely to Mrs. Goldspink. Even if he did see fit to withhold his fortune from his daughter, which he is not so lost to all family feeling to do, it would make little difference. Mrs. Goldspink is more than pleased with the match."

"So that's why Mrs. Goldspink was so changed," said Belle. "Poor soul, I feel sorry for her. No wonder she's been so suspicious, having to watch old Goldspink all the time. And what a wicked old thing he is. Fancy her letting him go home alone!"

"She had no option," said the Colonel, "and he's had a bad fright. I believe they had a most affectionate parting and he will no doubt be more careful in future."

"That explains the Goldspinks," said Belle. "Now the Sweetings. Why should Mrs. Sweeting come and say her piece?"

"To keep in with the Colonel, of course, stupid!" snapped Daisy. "Where would she be without the Orsett family to brag about?"

"But, according to her, Julia is going to marry most advantageously, although we don't know who."

"I think I can answer that," put in the Colonel. "Mrs. Sweeting has high hopes of Mr. Arbuthnot."

"Not Tubby!"

"No, not that young fool. His father."

"Gawd Almighty!" gulped Daisy. "Here, Nabbs," she called. "Come in here a minute. What do you think's the latest? That Sweeting woman has picked on old Mr. Arbuthnot for that girl."

Nabbs was properly astonished.

"But it wasn't tied up, was it?" continued Daisy suspiciously. "She was being a bit more cautious than she usually is."

"Frightened he'll slip the leash," ventured Nabbs.

"Mind you," said Daisy, "that girl's as pretty as a basketful of angels and no mistake."

"Serves the old fellow right for getting in the way all the time," said Nabbs. "Trying to save that young Tubby from any woman who half-looked in his direction, and now gets caught himself. Tell you what though," he added confidentially, "old Mr. A wouldn't do nothing without the Colonel's say-so. Never has. Sets great store by the Colonel's opinion."

"That explains it then," breathed Daisy. "Would you advise Mr. Arbuthnot, sir, that it would be a good thing for him to marry Miss Sweeting?"

"In certain circumstances I might," agreed the Colonel. "Do him good. Fellow's becoming a proper old woman."

Nabbs chuckled, an awesome sound. "I don't envy Mr. Arbuthnot his mother-in-law, that I don't!"

"Well, that's one thing you won't be able to throw up in my face," flashed Daisy. "My poor old mum died twenty years back!"

A vein throbbed ominously in the Colonel's forehead. "Will you two go and finish your flirtation outside, please?"

"I'm sorry, sir, but I cannot leave this room with my lady in bed and you practically in there with her, if I may say so sir, unchaperoned," objected Daisy, but Nabbs scooped her up and bore her off to the landing, kicking and squealing delightedly. The door closed.

"About that proposal," said Belle. Her cheeks were burning and she looked enchanting.

"Yes," said the Colonel.

"I proposed to you because I thought you were responsible for—you know. I didn't see why you should ruin my life and get off scot-free, so I proposed to get my own back! Now I know the truth, and anyway after all that fracas, well, I didn't mean it," she finished lamely.

The colonel looked down at her. "Sure?"

Belle went very red indeed and didn't answer.

"So I'm free, am I? You have no claim on me at all?"

"Yes, you're free. I have no claim on you."

"Excellent," said the Colonel. "Now perhaps I can proceed with my courtship in my own way instead of the cackhanded manner in which you have mismanaged everything so far. I may say I was outraged at being proposed to. Now you can see what happens when women try to usurp the male prerogatives. I have been put to considerable loss of time and temper at a period when I can ill-afford to lose either. Not only with the Goldspinks and Sweetings either. I had the devil of a scene with Melton when I gave him notice to quit."

"The house in Berkeley Square?"

"The same."

"It's yours?"

"Not that you'd know it. They've been living there for years and the rent is always overdue. I don't mind that, but I do object to it when his wife starts meddling with my affairs."

"What did he say?" whispered Belle.

"It was all damned depressing, damned depressing," said the Colonel. "In the end, I had to relent, provided my future wife agreed."

"Oh," said Belle. Well, that accounted for the Meltons. "Mr. Lawton came 'round too, quite in his element that he was so much in demand by the aristocracy."

"Another fool," snorted the Colonel.

"He was very nice to me," tried Belle. "He apologized all over the place and he brought me those flowers."

The Colonel gave the innocent blooms a withering look. "Damned impudence!'

Belle snuggled closer.

"I have no doubt," said the Colonel, "that my proposal will seem boringly old-fashioned but I *am* boringly old-fashioned so you will have to make the best of it." He cleared his throat. "Miss Barclay—"

"When you said about taking *extreme measures,* you meant then that you were going to ask me to marry you, didn't you?" chipped in Belle.

The Colonel breathed heavily. "Yes. We got interrupted and no further occasion presented itself. From the racket on those stairs, I don't know if it's presented itself now."

"I thought so, but I wasn't sure," said Belle.

"Then, if I may continue? Thank you. Miss Barclay—"

But the door crashed open yet again and Mrs. Kimmence announced in ringing tones, and to the manner born, "Her Grace, the Duchess of Peckham!"

"GORE! Get up off your knees this instant!" came the well-remembered tones of the Duchess. "And as for you, my gel! You can stop that, d'you hear? I'm not having you play fast and loose with my son. Gore's a good lad and I will not have his life and his parliamentary career ruined by a tuppeny-hapenny actress, d'you hear? And I thought you was a *nice* gel!"

"Mama! Do you mind?"

'Yes, I do mind," quivered the Duchess venemously.

Oh, well, I might have known it was too good to last, thought Belle philosophically. *Whatever she pretends, the*

Colonel is the apple of her eye. Far more so than Hugo. Of course she would hate him marrying me. She opened her eyes.

The Duchess was supported by a stick and was a bit breathless but was otherwise in pretty good shape for a nonagenarian who had just climbed two flights of breakneck stairs. Temper had evidently endowed the Duchess' legs with a new lease of life, for a right temper she was in. Her black curls shook with it, her black eyes snapped with it, the jet fringes on her old-fashioned dress quaked with it.

"You—you—*wicked* gel!" she fumed, waving her stick at Belle. "You wicked little 'ussy!"

"How did you find your way here, Mama?" asked the Colonel.

"I made inquiries as I always have to if I want to know what's happening in my own family," answered his parent. "Lucky I did. If I hadn't, I shouldn't have heard from you until it was too late, and the damage done."

"Please, my lady!" begged Belle tearfully. "I'm not going to marry your son. I know it wouldn't do."

"Oh yes you will, you—you *minx!* If you don't I shall have you *summonsed,* d'you hear? Summonsed! I won't have my son jilted. You'll marry him and no more nonsense about it!"

"But—"

"Come to my house he did, nearly out of his mind. Never saw the lad so agitated."

"Mama!"

"I soon got it all out of him. Got it into his head that you might have come to me when you ran away from the Park. 'She'd never dare show her face here,' I said to him. 'Jilt you and then come whining to me?' "

"I didn't jilt him!"

"Don't you dare to contradict me, miss! You did. Got engaged to him, didn't you? Told everyone, then walked out on him. Not so much as a note where you were. Lad looked a fool. I won't have my son looking a fool. Worth twenty of you."

"All right," said Belle, after a short silence. "I'll marry him."

"And so I should hope," said the Duchess.

"Now, Mama," said the Colonel with ominous calm. "If you would be so good as to wait outside for a few minutes, I will personally conduct you home."

"Well, hurry up then," ordered the Duchess suspiciously. "And if you want a ring—" She began tugging an enormous emerald off one of her fingers.

"Thank you. I am already provided with one," returned the Colonel, propelling the old lady towards the door.

"Where did you get it?"

"Asprey's."

"I suppose it's all right then," said the Duchess reluctantly.

"I'm sure it will be adequate. Nabbs! Look after Her Grace, please. God Almighty, is the whole district assembled on these stairs?" demanded the Colonel irritably.

He slammed the door shut but failed to notice, as Belle did, that it immediately opened again furtively, and the heads of the Duchess, Nabbs, Daisy, the Kimmences and Mrs. Tovee could be half discerned, one over the top of the other, in the opening. A breathless silence fell.

The Colonel advanced towards the bed. "I will try again," he announced. "Miss Barclay, I have long admired your beauty and vivacity, but for several weeks past this feeling towards you has ceased to be one of mere warm regard and has become deepened and enriched into a devotion and, I may say, adoration which I find hard to express in words. Dare I hope that your own feelings towards me are not entirely those of indifference? If they are not, and you will be—"

"Mmmm!" mumbled Belle agreeably, and fell fast asleep in his arms.

Jean Plaidy

"Miss Plaidy is also, of course, Victoria Holt." —PUBLISHERS WEEKLY

☐ BEYOND THE BLUE MOUNTAINS	22773-1	1.95
☐ CAPTIVE QUEEN OF SCOTS	.23287-5	1.75
☐ THE CAPTIVE OF KENSINGTON PALACE	23413-4	1.75
☐ THE GOLDSMITH'S WIFE	. 22891-6	1.75
☐ HERE LIES OUR SOVEREIGN LORD	23256-5	1.75
☐ LIGHT ON LUCREZIA	23108-9	1.75
☐ MADONNA OF THE SEVEN HILLS	23026-0	1.75

A-33